LP   Edwards, Rachelle
STORAGE   Runaway Bride
EDWARDS

D1774530

Runaway Bride
LP EDWARDS
39204000025349
Edwards, Ra
Gilpin County Public Library

RUNAWAY BRIDE

Rachelle Edwards

G.K.HALL &CO.
Boston, Massachusetts
1991

LP
EDWARDS

Copyright © 1982 by Rachelle Edwards.

All rights reserved under International and Pan-American Copyright Conventions.

Published in Large Print by arrangement with Robert Hale Limited.

G. K. Hall Large Print Book Series.

Set in 16 pt. Plantin.

Library of Congress Cataloging-in-Publication Data

Edwards, Rachelle.
    Runaway bride / Rachelle Edwards.
       p.   cm.—(G.K. Hall large print book series) (Nightingale series)
   ISBN 0-8161-5155-5 (large print)
   1. Large type books. I. Title.
[PR6055.D948R86   1991]
823'.914—dc20   90-25126

One

A solitary rider galloped up the birch grove as it straightened to give a view of the elevated site of Birchwood House. It was a modest country house, built in the classical manner from local stone, and was considered by all who came upon it to be handsome. In front of the house nothing marred the view of lawns and trees which stretched for several miles.

At the sight of three carriages standing in front of the canopied portico the rider slowed somewhat, allowing the groom who had been following to catch up at last.

The rider, a young woman of some twenty years, clad in a bottle green habit and hat which sat atop her auburn curls, slowed her horse to almost a canter as she gazed in dismay at the escutcheon of Lord Frampton which adorned the door of one of the carriages. The other, a splendid affair with yellow paint and plush leather upholstery, she recognised also, this one belonging to her step-father, Sir Hector Liddell.

As was her usual custom when riding alone, the girl sat astride her mare like a man, and there were few who were her equal at horsemanship. Before the groom could come to her side she had dismounted unaided, thrusting the reins into his hands. Almost absent-mindedly she patted the horse's neck as it snorted and steamed in the cool afternoon air. Her pleasure at such an invigorating ride had disappeared the moment she had clapped eyes on the carriages.

After some considerable hesitation and only after the groom had begun to lead away the horses, she walked slowly up the steps and into the hall as if dreading what she might find. However, apart from two footmen it was deserted and, catching her breath, the girl gathered up her skirts and began to hurry up the stairs.

She had gone but a few steps when the library door opened. The sound of it caused her to flinch slightly. Although she hesitated she did not turn, hoping she would not be seen, but it was a faint hope.

"Clarinda!" cried a familiar voice. "Clarinda, my dear, do you not wish to welcome me home?"

At the sound of his voice she turned on her heel to face her step-father who was standing in the doorway of the library, looking mightily pleased with himself. Fleetingly, she wondered if he had, by way of a change, won a few guineas at the gaming tables.

She forced a smile to her lips although welcome was the last thing she wished him.

"Good day to you, Sir Hector."

He laughed in a good-natured way which she did not trust. "Is that all you have to say after so long a parting?"

Clarinda's manner did not alter. "I trust you had a comfortable journey."

"Indeed, we did."

She cast him a look of disdain; his cheeks were florid from too much drink, his shirt collar overstarched and exaggerated in its style. He could scarcely turn his head, so high were the points of his collar, and his coat was too wide at the shoulders to be elegant, and, adorned by large paste buttons, it would be certain to offend anyone who declared himself an arbiter of fashion.

Sir Hector eyed her speculatively. "You appear to be in rude health, my dear."

"Yes, I thank you."

He hesitated a moment longer, perhaps awaiting a further comment from her, before he went on, "You will be delighted to learn that we have a guest."

Her head came up. "Indeed?"

"Lord Frampton has accompanied me for a short stay . . ."

"So I noted. By your leave, Sir Hector."

She turned to continue up the stairs and as she did so he said in a more resolute voice, "Perchance you will join us when you have changed out of your riding clothes." Clarinda was about to declare the onset of a headache, but before she could do so he went on, in an almost cajoling tone of voice, "I have news which might cause you some pleasure."

She cast him a curious glance but she caught sight of only a satisfied smile as he returned to the library and closed the door. She remained motionless for a few moments longer, considering what he had said, before the sound of raucous laughter from the library sent her running up the stairs at last.

As she washed away the grime of her ride she reflected that little her step-father might say or do would cause her pleasure. She had disliked him from the outset, and with good reason. His careless attitude towards her late mother had always irked, and beneath that dissipated exterior she was quite convinced there lurked an unscrupulous man.

To her mind there was nothing more unpleasant than joining him and Lord Frampton for the evening, but she could find no alternative to doing so. It was always possible to feign that headache after all and cry off joining him and his equally loathsome crony, but Clarinda was not a girl to be so faint-hearted. She knew that she would have to face them eventually. She could only hope that their stay would be, as usual, a short one. Rusticating did not suit them and as before the gambling halls and bawdy houses of London always beckoned temptingly.

As her maid hooked her into a peach-coloured velvet gown, the girl said, "You'll be glad Sir Hector's back, ma'am."

At that moment such a tactless remark was the last thing required, causing Clarinda to bite back a sharp retort. However she did curb her tongue, for Hetty had been her maid for only a short time. Since her mother's death all but the most elderly and loyal of their servants had left Birchwood House, allowing Sir Hector to replace them with people of his own choosing. Clarinda suspected that the maid was on more than familiar terms with her step-father, which did not endear the girl to her mistress.

"I doubt if he will remain for long. He never does. The attractions of Town are all too inviting for him to stay away."

"Ah, but while he's here, ma'am, the house is not so empty."

Clarinda sat down at her dressing table and allowed Hetty to pin and dress her long tresses, long since acknowledged as her best feature apart from her wide green eyes. The maid was good with her hands, Clarinda had to grant her that.

"I have no complaints about the house being empty; I rather like the solitude."

"Not natural, that. When you're wed, ma'am, you'll have a houseful, that's for sure."

"Married?" Clarinda echoed, starting slightly. "Oh, I doubt if I shall be married for a long while."

Hetty shrugged and pointed out, "Most ladies of the Quality are already wed at your age, ma'am."

Irritated now, Clarinda retorted, "They,

no doubt, have a London Season to enable them to meet suitable young men. My mother's illness and death ended that possibility and there is no one else who might invite me to Town."

"Well, it's not always necessary, is it?" Hetty answered soothingly. "There are gentlemen more close at hand."

Clarinda cast her a sharp look through the mirror. "I think you go too far. I don't wish to discuss such a matter with you. Please don't mention it again."

Hetty lowered her eyes. "I beg your pardon, ma'am," she said in a servile way which Clarinda did not entirely trust.

After a few moments' silence Clarinda could not help but say, "'Tis obvious you are glad Sir Hector is returned."

"Indeed I am, ma'am, as all the servants are, you may be sure. It is always good when the master's at home."

Clarinda contrived to control her ire but she silently vowed to dismiss the impudent doxy as soon as she was able to do so. She stood up abruptly.

"That will be all, Hetty, and I shan't be needing you again tonight."

The girl lowered her eyes respectfully.

"As you wish, ma'am," and hurried out of the room.

Her mistress watched her go with scarcely concealed resentment and then she snatched up her shawl and needlework before going downstairs.

Her step-father and his friend, Lord Frampton, were still ensconced in the library and the moment she entered it was evident to her that they had consumed a good deal of claret in her absence. They seemed to be in rollicking spirits, but that did not hearten her.

However as the footman closed the door behind them Lord Frampton put down his brimming glass and came across the room, taking her hand in his immediately.

"Miss Devereaux, what a pleasure to see you again, and looking so robust. Rusticating becomes you, ma'am."

"Mayhap Town living would do so even more. I cannot know."

For some reason he chuckled before saying, "And your gown, I am bound to say, is most becoming. Is it not, Liddell?"

"Clarinda always exhibits the most gracious taste."

"It is an old one, my lord," she answered,

disengaging her hand as soon as politely possible.

It had always been so; Lord Frampton took every opportunity of touching her and Clarinda loathed his proximity, always escaping it as soon as she might.

She walked away from him, disliking the smell of his cologne which seemed to assail her senses. He, too, was dressed in a similar fashion to Sir Hector. His breeches fitted so tightly they were constantly wrinkled and she wondered that he could sit down in them.

He escorted her to a sofa where she immediately became engrossed in her embroidery, hoping he would not insist upon joining her.

To her relief he did not; he and Sir Hector exchanged glances before her step-father asked, "Clarinda, my dear, would you care for a glass of claret? It really is an excellent wine."

She looked up briefly. "I should not doubt it as you tolerate only the best liquor, but no, I thank you."

"You are very abstemious," Lord Frampton commented, taking up his own glass and draining it.

"If that is so it is only because I have seen

the effects of too much indulgence in others."

Lord Frampton cleared his throat, looking a mite discomfited. "You must be lonely here when Sir Hector is in London. This house is so large for one," he laughed gruffly, "as dainty as you, my dear."

"It is because it is so big that I am well occupied, my lord." She looked up briefly and cast them both an acid smile. "Servants today are so unreliable, and downright lazy. I am occupied almost constantly ensuring that all the work is done in a satisfactory manner."

Lord Frampton laughed again. "Judging by the condition of Birchwood House, I am persuaded you succeed admirably, my dear."

He put down his empty claret glass, glancing at Sir Hector with rather less gaiety than before. "With your permission I believe I shall go and ensure that my own servant has unpacked my belongings properly before we go in to dinner. No doubt," he added, rubbing his hands together, "it will be, as usual, an excellent repast."

When he had gone Clarinda could not resist adding, "He could not judge if it were not."

Surprisingly, her remark caused Sir Hector to laugh. "One would almost conclude you did not like Lord Frampton." He paused and when she made no comment, he added in a soft voice, "He is exceedingly fond of you."

Her embroidery needle jabbed into her finger which she immediately sucked. Then, as a stain of blood spread over the canvas, she said, "I did not look to see you here so soon."

"The charms of London easily pall, and I am exceedingly fond of Birchwood."

"I am surprised, I own, to hear you say so. Perchance Mrs. Cuthbert and Mrs. Egmont are not in residence in Town at the present time."

His face became even redder and she knew she was treading on dangerous ground to goad him so. Even so, Clarinda gained a flutter of pleasure at the response she had elicited at the mention of his lightskirts. A spark of anger could easily be detected in his eyes but a moment later he was all affability once more.

He walked away from her. "You must have your little jest, my dear. I know you are for ever roasting me, but you must have a care lest your humour is misinterpreted by those who do not know or love you as well as I do." He turned to face her again. There was a smile on his lips but she noted that his eyes were cold. "Do you recall I mentioned I had some pleasing news for you?"

Artless again, she answered, "I had quite forgotten, but no doubt you will seek to remind me."

"Lord Frampton," he said slowly and with no small amount of satisfaction, "has sought my permission to marry you." He paused to allow her to digest his news and as she stared at him wide-eyed, he added, "Naturally, I have been most pleased to give my consent."

At this news Clarinda thrust aside her needlework with a shaking hand and was immediately on her feet.

"Marry me? Lord Frampton?" she gasped.

He laughed. "Such modesty. You are delightful, but you cannot pretend you are not aware of his regard for you. He has displayed it of late most plainly."

"You cannot think I would accept. I will not!"

The satisfied smile became a little stiffer.

"My dear Clarinda, you cannot know the honour you are being accorded."

"I know I have never been so shocked in my life."

"An understandable reaction."

"You do not understand; I do not wish to marry Lord Frampton. I would not wish to marry him if he were the last man left alive on earth!"

He stroked his chin and averted his face. "I am persuaded that once you have had time to think on this matter you will declare yourself delighted."

"I most certainly will not! And I have no intention of marrying him."

"Clarinda, don't get into a pucker over this. You must allow me to know what is best for you. You are very young and cannot know what is best for yourself."

"If I live to be ninety I shall not change my mind."

He leaned back against the desk and folded his arms, gazing at her as she stared back at him defiantly. No trace of his good humour remained and it was all she could do not to tremble. If she had not been so outraged she would have felt fear.

"You are too headstrong for your own good, Clarinda. I should have taken you to task earlier; I can see that now. However, in this matter I will brook no argument. You are not yet of age and your sainted mother entrusted your guardianship to me."

"Oh, you hypocrite!" she cried, beyond all reason now that her mother's name had been mentioned. "How dare you speak of Mama. You and your cronies, basket-scramblers all of them, squandered her fortune and were so busy doing so you could not drag yourself away from the arms of your doxy to attend her when she was dying."

The colour once again rose in his cheeks and he straightened up. At the same time his hand shot out and caught her on the cheek. Clarinda gasped with pain and shock as she staggered back from the force of it.

"How dare you?" she gasped, cradling her enflamed cheek in the palm of her hand.

"I should have sought to chastise you long ago, madam. You are too top-lofty for your own good. At your age you should be glad of an opportunity to marry at all, let alone a title."

"A bankrupt one."

"Be silent, madam!"

He slapped her again, this time on the other cheek, and she fell back against the desk. As she nursed her stinging cheeks he said in a more cajoling voice, "Clarinda, my dear, this is unseemly and so unnecessary."

Slowly she straightened up and fixed him with a hate-filled look. "You must be as cunning as a dead pig to think I haven't guessed what you're about. No doubt you and your crony are in dun territory and you're in need of my fortune to settle your bills. I wouldn't be up to snuff if I didn't guess what you're scheming between you. Well, it won't work, for I shan't marry him whatever you do. I'm not such a buffle-head as you suppose."

She marched purposefully towards the door.

"Impudent hussy!" he roared, beyond all reason now. "How dare you disdain such an offer?"

When she continued towards the door he came after her, catching hold of her arm and swinging her round to face him again. His grip made her wince but she would not let him see he had hurt her yet again.

"Please unhand me," she asked in a low and slightly uneven voice.

"Not until you vow to obey me and I do

mean to enforce my decision, you may be certain."

Her head came up proudly. "In this I never will. I loathe Lord Frampton and I will never marry him."

Through his teeth he answered, "We shall see."

She tore away from his grip once more, but just as she was about to pull open the door he reached for one of his walking sticks and lashed out at her with it. The blow flung her against the wall, all but knocking the breath from her body. As she groped for some purchase to right herself he hit her again and she cried out in pain and fear.

"You have been nursed in cotton for too long, my girl," he breathed as he struck out at her repeatedly. "It is time you learned what it is to obey, in a manner you can understand."

From the tone of his voice she thought he sounded glad of the opportunity but that was before he hit her again, mercilessly despite her cries. Although she struggled to escape him it was to no avail for oblivion soon became a merciful release.

Two

The bedroom door opened slowly to admit a sliver of light.

"Miss Devereaux."

At the sound of Hetty's voice Clarinda moved slightly and then groaned at the effort it cost her.

The maid came further into the room. "Miss Devereaux, Sir Hector sent me up to attend you. He says you had an accident." When she made no answer the maid asked, "Shall I mend the fire?"

"No," Clarinda managed to gasp at last. Her lips were swollen and speech was difficult. "I am quite all right. Go away, do."

"It's grown so dark; shall I light a candle afore I do?"

"No! Just . . . go away."

Suddenly the maid caught sight of Clarinda in the glow coming from the embers of the fire and her eyes opened wide.

"Miss Devereaux!"

"Go away, Hetty."

"But your face! You must have fallen very badly to hurt yourself so . . ."

"Fallen?"

"Aye, into the hearth. Do you not recall?"

"No."

"Sir Hector told me what happened. Tripped on the rug, you did, but I never thought you'd be so bad. Shall I send Arthur for a physician? If he goes now he'd be back by mornin'."

"No, I'm all right. I need no physician. I just want to sleep. See I am . . . not disturbed. I . . . have taken some . . . laudanum."

"Very well, ma'am," the maid replied, but she still sounded doubtful.

"Go back to what you were doing."

Despite her pain and misery Clarinda could not resist the rejoinder and imagined the colour creeping up the girl's cheeks.

As soon as the door had closed, Clarinda eased herself painfully from the bed. She was wearing only her shift and could scarce recall dragging herself upstairs and taking off her gown.

After pausing for a few moments to catch her breath she staggered to the dressing table and lit a candle. Holding it up to the mirror she could then see what had shocked Hetty so. Her face was a mass of bruises and lacerations. At the sight of them she closed her eyes, blotting out the hideous mess and she knew all too well it would look even worse by morning.

However, her pain and marred appearance was not the real worry which plagued her. Marriage to Lord Frampton was a fate she couldn't bear to contemplate. As she sank down into a chair her despair was more painful than her injuries. Her heart overflowed with hatred for Sir Hector and she vowed at that moment to have her revenge upon him one day, not only for her own humiliation, but for the injustices he had done her mother.

Despairingly she was aware he could easily force her to marry Lord Frampton who would then have control of the fortune her father had left in trust for her. She just couldn't let it happen.

With a very great effort she eased her aching body from the chair and went to the commode. Pulling out the top drawer she groped beneath a Paisley shawl. After a moment her fingers located what she was seeking and she drew out a leather purse. In the semi-darkness she counted the contents which came to the princely sum of seven guineas.

Drawing a sigh she realised it was not a

great deal of money but it would have to serve her needs. After wrapping her jewellery in a handkerchief (her mother's had long since disappeared) she went to the press and selected a riding habit and her warmest cloak.

It was with some difficulty that she dressed. Normally she was not called upon to do so without the help of a maid, but on this occasion not only did she have to contend with hooks and laces but there was not a part of her body which did not hurt abominably.

At last she was fully dressed, but she did not waste time putting up her hair. Wearing the cloak and with her valuables close to her skin she opened the door a fraction, cursing silently when it creaked. The corridor was deserted and no one could be heard moving around. Most of the servants would have retired by now and Clarinda was fairly certain Sir Hector and his crony would be quite foxed at this time of the night and no danger to her. However, she was determined to be prudent.

She pulled up the hood of her cloak to conceal her give-away hair and hurried down the corridor, not towards the main staircase but to the back one. One solitary candle was alight but it was sufficient for her to see where she was going.

A new moon lit her way to the stables as she crossed the lawn, as silent as a ghost. She paused once to glance back at the house, but no one stirred despite several lighted windows.

When she reached the stable block she paused again for fear anyone was still in there. As she listened she heard only the occasional whinnying of a restless horse.

Before going inside she glanced back at Birchwood once more. It looked black and menacing against the night sky. Somewhere near, an owl hooted and she started nervously. Birchwood had been her home for so long and there had been many happy hours within those walls. Her throat was constricted with emotion as she recalled them, but she vowed to return one day when Birchwood would be free of Sir Hector and full of laughter and happiness once more.

When she entered the stables more of the horses became restless but she knew that their noise would not be heard at the house. She glanced regretfully at her own mare, Bess, whom she had ridden so hard that day. It was difficult for Clarinda to leave her but she needed a mount which was rested and fresh. Unhesitatingly she went to Mungo.

With some difficulty she contrived to saddle him and then, going as carefully as she could, she led him out into the stable yard. It came as a relief to her that no one had so far heard but her stealth had meant she was taking an agonising amount of time. She longed to climb into the saddle and ride away at a gallop but she stifled the urge and led Mungo across the grass which muffled the sound of his hooves, and into the adjoining fields. Only then did she mount him and digging in her heels urged him into a gallop which would take her away from the home she loved as well as the man she hated.

The moon was on the wane, the sun lighting up the sky to the east. Only startled animals in the hedgerows stirred as Clarinda trudged along the uneven track, leading her lame horse.

Every now and again she glanced worriedly at the sky as daybreak approached fast. Clarinda knew that Sir Hector would not become aware of her absence for hours yet, but even so she needed to put as many miles between them as was possible. With a lame horse progress was impossible so if she did not find an inn soon and obtain a fresh mount he would easily catch up with her before the day was out.

Clarinda had lost count of how many miles she had travelled since starting out. She knew only that this was the London road and she must come across an inn before long.

All the while she fought pain and exhaustion, willing herself to go a little further, and then further still. She put one foot before the other almost automatically until she rounded a bend in the road. There at the roadside was a tempting stretch of turf. At this point she felt she deserved a short respite and, tying Mungo to a tree, she sank down to rest thankfully for a few minutes. She was, however, unprepared for the feeling of complete weariness which swept over her. Her eyes seemed to be closing of their own accord even though she fought to keep them open and eventually she did not trouble to struggle against the invading sleep any longer.

It was Mungo's whinnying which brought her back to wakefulness again. For a moment she expected to find herself in her own room and then with a start she recalled all that had happened.

The sun was quite high in the sky so it

was likely she had slept for a long time. Precious hours. As she struggled to sit up her body seemed to ache all the more. Her lips were stiffer than before and the cuts more sore. Never before had she felt so wretched.

The sorrowful feeling, however, was only a fleeting one, for a movement nearby caused her to sit up more quickly than she really should. She looked round in alarm and then struggled to her feet, for a group of people dressed in disreputable clothing were gathered around her horse discussing him vociferously.

"What do you think you're doing there?" she demanded, her heart fluttering with alarm.

One man who seemed to be the leader of the group detached himself from the others. He looked filthy and smelled far from wholesome. As he came closer to her she resisted the urge to back away, her head coming up in a proud gesture. He pushed his battered beaver hat to the back of his head and grinned, revealing a row of blackened teeth.

"Fine bit o' horseflesh, that, ma'am."

"Indeed it is. I don't need you to tell me that." His stare was such a blatant one she was forced to avert her eyes. "Who are all these people, anyway?"

"Travelling folk, we be."

"Gypsies," she answered in disgust, alarmed anew.

His eyes narrowed as he studied her. The others had also left Mungo and began to gather around Clarinda, and she did start to back away then.

"What's a gentry mort like you doing all alone on the high toby?"

"I am not . . . alone," she was quick to assure them. "My . . . brother has gone to look for lodgings. I . . . was too tired to go on—and, of course my horse has gone lame."

The gypsies continued to eye her speculatively which made her feel more nervous all the time.

"He is bound to be back any minute now," she added for good measure.

"Looks as if you've 'ad a mis'ap," one of the women pointed out.

Clarinda's hand went to her face. "It is nothing, I assure you. I merely . . . fell from my horse." Then she moved towards Mungo in a decisive manner. "You will have to excuse me; I must go."

"Ain't yer gonna wait for yer brother?" the leader asked, grinning wickedly.

"I shall walk on to meet him."

"Won't do yer 'orse any good. Tell yer what; I'll buy him from you for . . . say . . . a guinea."

Clarinda turned on her heel, outraged by his impudence. "A guinea! How dare you so much as suggest it. This is no daisy cutter. Mungo's a prime piece of blood."

"Ain't no good to you lame," he pointed out. "We'll give yer one o'ours so's yer can go on to meet yer brother."

She regarded their mangy beasts with disdain and then answered icily, "No, I thank you."

They'd begun to close in on her again, much to her alarm.

"In an 'urry, miss?" one of them asked.

"Yes," she answered breathlessly. "My brother and I have to be in London by the morrow. We have an audience with the Queen," she added.

This only resulted in laughter from the gypsies who began to skip around, curtseying to one another.

"Goin' to see the Queen, eh?" mocked an old crone, giving her an awkward curtsey. "My, my, we do 'ave a grand one 'ere, don't we?"

"We're goin' to London. Come wi' us," a woman invited. "Mayhap yer've some jewels you'd like us to sell for yer, a gentry mort like you?"

Clarinda's eyes opened wide with alarm. "I have none, none at all."

"No jewels when you meet the Queen," mocked the old crone. "What is the Quality comin' to?"

The others laughed at this and as they did so a hand reached out and stroked her hair which hung loose to her waist.

She flinched away as a youth cried, "Cor, look at 'er 'air. Like a camp fire, it is."

She began to back away from them once again. "You impudent coxcomb! Keep your hands to yourselves or my brother will whip you when he returns."

"But he ain't here," said the leader regretfully.

"Sell yer 'air to us, dearie?" the old crone asked. "Worth a penny or two, that is."

Clarinda's eyes grew wide and she choked back a cry of alarm, making ready to run from them even if it did mean leaving Mungo behind. In any event he could not carry her.

Suddenly, though, she heard the pounding of hooves on the road approaching fast. Only one horse, she reckoned quickly, so it could not be Sir Hector even if he had risen early, which was unheard of anyway.

"That must be my brother returning!" she cried triumphantly, dashing into the road.

As a solitary rider rounded the corner Clarinda waved her hands frantically in the air to stop him going past. He had been riding so fast he had to pull hard on the reins to halt his horse and the poor animal, seeing a cloaked figure dash in front of him, reared up, neighing angrily.

Clarinda's relief soon turned to alarm as a pair of flailing hooves hovered above her. She stepped back quickly and fell into a rut in the road. The horse seemed out of control, about to throw its rider and she closed her eyes and averted her face as the hooves bore down on her, to crush out all life beneath that powerful bulk.

Three

The sound of hooves continued to pound deafeningly inside Clarinda's head. When she could bear it no longer she cried out.

"Now, now," answered a soothing voice, "you've nought to fear now, m'dear."

At last she forced open her eyes to discover she was no longer on the open road and no worse injured than before. She was lying in a half tester bed very much like her own at Birchwood and her first thoughts were that she had been dreaming all the time.

It had all been a nightmare, she thought with profound relief. I am back at Birchwood and none of those awful events had happened after all.

That thought made her sit up immediately. It was then that she realised she was wearing a strange linen nightshift which was many sizes too large for her. The room, she now discovered, was totally different to her own at Birchwood; it was much smaller and cosier for one thing. The walls were panelled with dark oak. The floorboards, highly polished and covered only by a Turkey rug, creaked as someone walked across them.

"How do you be feelin', m'dear?"

As a stranger approached the other side of the bed, Clarinda turned her head sharply.

"I . . . am . . . feeling better, I thank you. Where . . . where am I? Who are you?"

"This be Cressfield Manor and I'm Mrs. Kellett, the housekeeper."

Clarinda gave the woman her attention, wondering what had happened to the gypsies and how she came to be sleeping in this strange bed.

The housekeeper, Clarinda judged, was past middleage, plump, and her rosy cheeks were those of a country woman. She seemed kind, and yet . . . Clarinda was not prepared to trust anyone entirely.

"Can you tell me what happened? How on earth did I get here? I don't recall it at all."

The housekeeper didn't reply immediately; she lifted a tray and offered the cup it bore to the invalid. Clarinda looked at it suspiciously. The cup was an elegant china one, which for some reason surprised her.

"'Tis only a cup of chocolate, m'dear. It'll

do you good. Drink it down afore it grows too cold."

Just at that moment the smell of the chocolate steaming in the cup was overwhelming and Clarinda recalled that she hadn't eaten since breakfast the day before. Even so she hesitated a moment longer before lifting the cup from the tray.

"Walkin' in front of an 'orse is a crack-brained thing to do."

With the cup of chocolate clutched in her hands Clarinda sank back against the pillows. "Of course, I remember it clearly now. The gypsies frightened me and I ran towards the rider."

"Aye. We reckoned that was the reason, and no wonder; steal the skin off your back they would, and no mistake."

At such a pronouncement Clarinda suddenly clutched one hand to her breast. "Oh, my purse!"

Mrs. Kellett went to the dressing table and lifted up the knotted handkerchief and the purse. "All there I dare say, miss, no thanks to those thieving gypsies, though."

Clarinda drew a heartfelt sigh of relief and a moment later asked, "What time is it?"

"Near enough three of the afternoon.

You've been here since ten o'clock this morning."

Three o'clock, she thought with a start. She had been there too long. By now Sir Hector was bound to have discovered her gone.

As the housekeeper went towards the door she said, "Stay abed as long as you wish, m'dear, but Colonel Pennington wishes to speak to you when you're ready to see him."

"Colonel Pennington?" Clarinda echoed.

"Aye. He's the master of Cressfield Manor."

"Was it his horse?"

The housekeeper nodded and for a few moments Clarinda digested this information. So her rescuer was a military gentleman. He was bound to want to question her and on hearing her story he would have no sympathy for her situation. No doubt he was old and gouty, too, and would surely side with Sir Hector, insisting upon turning her over to him.

She put down the half finished cup of chocolate and pulled back the counterpane. "I have rested enough. Would you be kind enough to bring my clothes, Mrs. Kellett? I won't trouble you further after that."

The woman came back to the bed, her eyes narrowed. "Are you quite certain you feel recovered enough to get up, ma'am? It's no trouble having you here. It's been long enough . . ."

Warmed by her concern, Clarinda smiled. "I am quite sure."

Mrs. Kellett still did not look convinced. "Well, you stay there anyway. I'll send up your clothes—they've been cleaned—and some water. Tell the girl if there's anything you're wanting."

When she had gone Clarinda got up anyway. She immediately came face to face with her own reflection in the cheval mirror. She looked grotesque. Her slim body was enshrouded in what was undoubtedly one of Mrs. Kellett's nightshifts and her face was still an ugly welter of cuts and bruises.

She turned away in disgust and went to look out of the window. Pretty chintz curtains had been drawn across it and Clarinda pulled them back to peer out of small-paned windows to see an expanse of lawn which gave way to a formal flower garden, old-fashioned but charming. However hard she tried she couldn't recall arriving there, and even worse she had no notion where she was now.

There came a knock at the door and Clarinda automatically drew back, afraid, and then the door opened. A fairhaired girl came in, smiling slightly, followed by an older maidservant who carried hot water in a large ewer.

"Me name's Kate," the girl said when the other maid had poured the water into a heavy bowl on a stand by the window. As she left the room the girl went on, "I've to look after you, miss. Mam says so."

"Mrs. Kellett?"

"Aye."

As she went to lay out the clothes she had been carrying Clarinda said, "I am certain you will contrive very well, Kate."

The girl blushed with pleasure and as Clarinda gratefully washed in the slightly scented water the maid reverently set out the brushes on the dressing table.

"Are you sure you're feeling well enough to be up, ma'am?"

"I am much recovered, I thank you."

"Lucky not to have been killed, Mam says," the girl informed her as she helped Clarinda to dress. "If Colonel Pennington wasn't such a good horseman you might well have been."

"What is he like, this Colonel Pennington?" Clarinda asked as the girl brushed her hair.

Idly she picked up one of the silver-backed brushes which bore the initials A.P.

"Oh, I scarce see him. Bit of a recluse, he is. When he's not out on the estate he's reading in the library. Mam says he's a good master. She's devoted to him."

Clarinda sighed. They were all loyal servants and it was evident she would find no one here prepared to defy him.

She turned to the girl at last. "Thank you so much, Kate. You've done very well, but you can go now. I should like to rest a while before I see anyone."

The girl put the brush down and sketched a curtsey. "As you wish, ma'am. Just ring when you've rested and I'll bring a dish of tea up to you."

After the maidservant had gone Clarinda waited for some moments before gathering up her belongings and secreting them in her shift once more. Flinging her cloak over her habit she went out into the corridor. From the doorway she could see the landing and knew the servants' staircase would be in the opposite direction.

At that time of the afternoon almost all the servants would be engaged in preparing for dinner, so she felt quite confident about escaping unseen. The only problem was finding her way to London. She no longer had any notion of where she might be or what direction she must take. However, uppermost in her mind was the need to leave Cressfield Manor before it was discovered that she was a runaway.

Once outside the house she looked around for sight of the stable block which fortunately was near at hand. She crossed the courtyard furtively and was glad to reach the stable unseen.

Mungo whinnyed as she entered and she went up to him, pressing her face close and stroking him gently.

"How glad I am to see you, Mungo."

The horse nuzzled her gently. After a moment she sighed. "I hate to leave you here but I have no choice. I only hope Colonel Pennington won't mind too much if I take one of his horses instead of you."

"I am persuaded he will take the gravest exception to it."

The sound of a man's voice caused her to gasp and to straighten up. As she stared in alarm over the horse's back she caught sight of a man who was leaning against the open stable door, gazing at her.

"Mungo is very valuable."

"And so are the other horses," he replied, his gaze unrelenting.

"It is not as you think. I . . . just wanted to see him, make certain he is safe and well."

"Your concern is commendable, but what kind of horsewoman are you to ride a horse until he's lame?"

She considered such criticism unfair and she stiffened. "It was not my fault, and in any event I have always been considered to have an excellent seat."

The man smiled crookedly although there was little mirth in it. "I do not doubt it and I am persuaded the horse will recover."

At last she came out of the stall, regarding him with interest for the first time. He was about thirty years of age, she judged, and his brown hair was worn short and curled carelessly in the fashionable manner. His brown riding coat was plain and elegant, his breeches unwrinkled, and his tasselled hessians gleaming.

His dark eyes surveyed her with scarce concealed amusement, something which irritated her. She was also concerned about who he might be—certainly not a servant—and if he was likely to prevent her leaving.

As he watched her, he held an ebony cane and all the while he was caressing the gold lion's head which served as a handle. She couldn't repress a shudder at the memory of Sir Hector beating her with a similar object.

"I was not about to steal a horse," she explained, somewhat lamely.

He raised one eyebrow. "No?"

She reacted angrily. "No!"

"I accept your word on that, ma'am."

"Indeed?" she asked imperiously. "And who might you be?"

"I am Brooke Pennington. Who are you?"

She was taken aback. "Pennington! Then you must be Colonel Pennington's son."

"I am the only Pennington who lives here."

Her eyes opened even wider. "*You* are Colonel Pennington?"

Still retaining his indolent air he bowed slightly. "At your service, ma'am."

"You already have been—those awful gypsies. I was terrified. What happened to them?"

"They were sent on their way. What were you doing there alone, in any event?"

She bit her lip. She had still not recovered

from the shock of not finding him old and gouty.

"Forgive me, Colonel Pennington, but I cannot tell you."

He was regarding her from beneath his lowered lashes. "And you haven't yet told me your name."

"I beg of you not to ask, sir. You have done me a kindness and I have one more to ask of you; the loan of a horse and I shall be on my way with no further ado."

"Ah, so you wish to *borrow* one."

Her humility was on a short leash and irritation burned away inside her. However, of necessity she struggled to contain it.

"For a short time only."

"Where are you bound?" When she did not answer he went on, "Come now, you can surely answer that simple question." No answer was forthcoming and he said rather more irritably now, "This is exceeding odd to me, ma'am. You are obviously a lady of quality and yet you were abroad on the King's highway with no form of escort or protection. You cannot be eloping alone and there are your injuries to account for."

"Caused by my encounter with your horse," she answered quickly.

"Merlin did not touch you. You fainted, that is all."

Clarinda swallowed. "You must not ask, Colonel Pennington," she reiterated, "for I cannot tell you."

"If you cannot tell me, I cannot help you."

"You can indeed, for all I ask is to be sent on my way. That should not be too difficult. I don't wish to inconvenience you any further."

"How thoughtful of you," he answered sarcastically, which caused her anger to kindle once again.

It was abominable for her to think she was at the mercy of this horrid, sarcastic man, having to beg his help in so humiliating a manner.

Whilst Clarinda fought with her anger he took out his gold hunter, glanced at it briefly before putting it back in his waistcoat pocket. As he did so he cast her a speculative look.

"It will be dark in two hours' time and you have already encountered enough terrors for one day. Remain as my guest until the morrow and I vow you will be sent on your way in my carriage."

At so unexpected an offer she stared at

him with uncertainty. Aware of her doubts he went on, "I cannot force you to tell me what you are about, but I am certain you must be greatly afraid of something or someone. The man who inflicted such injuries is indeed a scoundrel, but let me assure you that you have nothing to fear from anyone at Cressfield Manor."

Suddenly her eyes swam with tears and her throat was choked. She swayed slightly and caught hold of the stable door. "Oh, Colonel Pennington, I . . ."

"Come," he said briskly, straightening up at last, "have dinner with me and I promise we shall only converse upon subjects of your own choice. It is a long time since I have had company here."

She walked out of the stable and when she glanced back she was both shocked and surprised to discover that his cane was not merely a fashionable accessory. He was leaning on it heavily and walked with a pronounced limp.

Her involuntary gasp caused him to look at her with narrowed eyes. "You are obviously shocked."

"I . . . did not . . . expect . . ."

"I trust I do not offend you."

"No, no, of course you do not. I was . . .

merely taken aback. I am truly sorry. 'Tis not . . . gout?"

He laughed softly. "Would that it was so, ma'am. This is a permanent reminder of Vimeiro."

"You fought in the Peninsula?"

"I was on Wellesley's personal staff until a French bullet put an end to that. Now I am obliged to live as a country gentleman whilst my comrades still fight and die."

"What a blessing Boney was trounced by the Russians. They say the war cannot last much longer."

"Let us hope that is so, ma'am."

"My step-father was in the army," she said, unwittingly revealing a fact.

He looked at her with interest and she said quickly, "He resigned his commission after his marriage."

"Manoeuvres on the downs are not the same as real battles and I fear some men find the difference too marked for comfort."

She was relieved when he did not insist upon questioning her further. They had come back to the house which Clarinda now noted was a Jacobean manor, half timbered with small-paned windows which appeared uneven and probably were. It was by no means a large house, but it did possess a great deal of charm and none of the orderly beauty of Birchwood.

"I trust you will not feel the need to run off again this evening," he said when they came into the hall.

She smiled shyly and shook her head, for all of her anger towards him had melted. "I am glad enough of the sanctuary you are offering me."

"Dinner will be served in an hour's time. You might like to rest until then."

At that moment she was reluctant to take her leave of him, feeling curious as to his circumstances, for there was something about him which caught her interest. Inevitably, though, she smiled and went up the stairs. When she had reached the landing she heard one of the downstairs doors closing.

Back in her room Clarinda vainly attempted to put up her hair, knowing she looked ridiculously young when it was down. Accustomed to Hetty's ministrations, she failed and contented herself by brushing it until it gleamed like the embers of the fire. When she had finished she turned the brush over in her hand, gazing at the ornate silver backing, A.P. Mother or wife? she wondered.

Not a wife, she decided immediately. He had said he didn't often enjoy company, which indicated a lonely existence.

Resting her elbows on the dressing table Clarinda became thoughtful again, her mind returning to her meeting with Brooke Pennington. He was certainly different to any of the bluff military men she had met previously. She supposed that the length of the war against Bonaparte had resulted in much younger men achieving high rank in the army. He looked as if he might once have been quite a Corinthian and in any event she guessed there would be few activities that damaged leg would prevent him pursuing.

It was a very long time since anyone had done her a genuine kindness and the sanctuary he offered, be it only for one night, was more than welcome. A meal, a clean bed and safety were of greater value just then than any fortune. And of equal importance, he had offered to send her on her way in a carriage, perhaps with an escort, too. She could scarcely believe her good fortune.

A knock on the door broke into her deep

thoughts and a moment later Kate came into the room.

"Excuse me, ma'am, but is there anything I can do for you?"

Decisively Clarinda answered, "If only you could put up my hair for me, Kate, I would be more than grateful."

"I'll try, ma'am," the girl answered with delight.

Try she certainly did and the result was delightful. She dressed Clarinda's heavy tresses into clusters of curls held in place by some tortoiseshell pins she had found in the dressing table.

"Such lovely hair," Kate crooned as she worked.

"And you have transformed it. Some gypsies wanted to buy it from me this morning."

"Buy it!" Kate cried. "They'd have cut it off with no more than a by your leave, ma'am."

Suddenly Clarinda groaned and Kate said in dismay, "You don't like it after all."

"Oh, I do, truly," Clarinda assured her, "only it's my face. There is nothing, I fear, you can do about that."

"You mustn't mind, ma'am. It will soon be mended. You're sound in limb after all."

"You are so full of good sense, Kate."

The girl blushed with pleasure and when, somewhere, a clock struck the hour Clarinda got to her feet.

"Colonel Pennington will be waiting for me and I know military men dislike unpunctuality."

As she walked towards the staircase she felt unaccountably nervous. Twenty-four hours earlier she had no notion of the strange turn of events which was to occur, and yet here she was in this house, her life changed utterly. It would never be the same again.

She was just about to go down the stairs when a loud pounding at the thick oak door caused her to draw back in alarm into the shadows of the landing.

Her heart was beating fast when a footman came to open the door. As it swung open she flinched even further into the shadows, for the voice which addressed the servant was one she recognised all too well. Her flight had been a fruitless one after all. Frustration and fear tore at her heart and she sank back in despair against the wainscoting, waiting for the inevitable discovery by her step-father who strode into the hall followed by Lord Frampton.

Four

Clarinda pushed her fist into her mouth to prevent a cry of alarm escaping her lips. Every fibre of her being trembled, for even if she contrived to escape the house down the back stairs, her step-father would soon catch up with her. To remain would only result in a humiliating conclusion to her spirited escape, for on hearing Sir Hector's story Colonel Pennington would have no alternative but to hand her back into his keeping.

Sir Hector threw back his caped riding coat and handed the lackey his card.

"Pray inform your master that I am come on urgent business."

A few moments passed, during which Clarinda's mind worked on countless useless solutions to her predicament. If only she had insisted on leaving whilst she had had the opportunity there would have been at least a small chance of evading him.

Whilst he waited, unaware of the watcher on the landing, Sir Hector paced the hall restlessly. "It's as if she has disappeared from the face of the earth," he muttered.

"I don't believe she can have got this far," Lord Frampton answered. "No one has seen her so we are merely wasting our time."

"Do not assume because she is a woman she cannot have ridden this far. The chit is a damned good horsewoman."

"It is more like she is lying injured or dead somewhere close to Birchwood."

"If only I could be certain of that, Bart. It would be a splendid solution to this problem."

Lord Frampton laughed softly. "And I should not be obliged to become leg-shackled to that branding iron."

It was all Clarinda could do not to rush down and berate them for their heartlessness.

"I thought you had a fondness for the chit," Sir Hector said in some surprise.

"I do. She is fetching, is she not? And of tender years. What man of spirit would not find her delectable, but when I am in funds there are others of a similar stamp with whom I can find solace without becoming leg-shackled."

They both laughed but then grew silent again when one of the doors opened and Colonel Pennington came limping into the hall. Sir Hector drew himself up to full height.

"Colonel Pennington, I believe."

Brooke Pennington glanced at Sir Hector's calling card. "Sir Hector Liddell."

"And this is the Earl of Frampton."

Colonel Pennington inclined his head, asking, "How may I be of service to you gentlemen?"

There was, she noted, no welcome in his manner. That at least was something.

"I regret having to disturb you, sir, at this hour." Her step-father stopped abruptly. "Colonel Pennington? Have we not met before, sir?"

"I think not."

"You did not serve with General Hoskins in the Peninsula?"

"No. Sir Hector, what is your business?"

"My apologies. We digress. We have the distressing duty to be in search of my step-daughter, Clarinda Devereaux."

Colonel Pennington took out his timepiece and looked at it pointedly. "What is that to me?"

Sir Hector looked outraged. "She may be here."

The younger man gazed at him icily. "Indeed?"

"She has absconded, sir, and we are concerned for her safety abroad alone."

"Quite understandable, but I am still not clear what this has to do with me."

"We are enquiring at every house we come to."

"I'm sorry I cannot be of help to you. I know of no one of that name."

The two men were already backing towards the door when Colonel Pennington asked, "Why did she abscond?"

Sir Hector looked surprised and then he smiled. "Who knows what foolish notions come into a girl's mind? The chit has windmills in her head and has been increasingly difficult since her Mama died. She is a sore trial to me."

"My commiserations, Sir Hector."

The baronet nodded and as he reached the door hesitated. "Colonel Pennington, are you certain we have not met before?"

"Not as far as I am aware, Sir Hector."

At this her step-father appeared satisfied and nodding again he strode out followed by the earl. As the footman closed the door Clarinda collapsed against the wall, feeling quite ill with relief. Colonel Pennington remained in the hall until the sound of their hoofbeats had faded into the distance and then he turned on his heel. Without looking up he said, "Miss Devereaux, you can come out now. They will not come back."

Shaken anew at the realisation he had known she was there all the time she came slowly down the stairs.

"Behind those weals and bruises you have gone quite pale," he told her with obvious amusement.

"You did not betray me," she answered breathlessly and in awe.

"I told him I knew of no one called Clarinda Devereaux and until you answered to that name a moment ago I had no notion that you were."

Her eyes glowed with pleasure and gratitude. "You are very kind."

His look of amusement faded. "Did you really think I would hand you over to a man who could inflict such injuries, or was some other person the culprit?"

She shook her head and he went on briskly, "Come, dinner is growing cold and my cook is too skilled to have her efforts treated with so much disdain."

As he ushered her towards the dining room she said, averting her face, "I look hideous. I only wonder you can bear to look at me."

A footman held out her chair as he took his place at the other end of the oak table. Two candelabra stood between them, casting light on to the damask covered walls.

"Ladies are always so concerned about their appearance. If you can abide my ugliness, I can surely tolerate yours. In any event," he went on before she could protest that it wasn't so, "your ugliness will fade soon enough, and no doubt a beauty lurks beneath."

Relieving her embarrassment the servants handed around the dishes containing beef, fowl and fish, all of which emitted tempting aromas. Clarinda helped herself from each dish, for she suddenly discovered she was ravenously hungry.

When she had eaten sufficient to satisfy her hunger she sat back at last to discover Colonel Pennington had long since finished and was watching her. Her cheeks grew red and at last she was glad of the bruises which hid her embarrassment.

"You must think me a glutton, Colonel Pennington."

"Obviously you have not eaten for a long while. Please feel free to eat more if you wish. Far too much is wasted."

She shook her head. "I am quite full, I thank you. You have an excellent cook."

"She will be glad to know you think so."

"From all I have observed, you have an excellent household."

"Thank you."

She wished she could be sure he wasn't mocking her comments.

"You live here alone, I note," she went on a moment later.

"Yes," he answered heavily.

"Then those brushes Kate used must have once belonged to your mother."

"No, my mother never lived here. They belonged to my wife, just as those pins you are wearing in your hair were hers. She died almost four years ago."

Almost involuntarily his gaze strayed to a painting of a beautiful woman which graced the wall over the server.

"She was very beautiful," Clarinda murmured.

"Thomas Lawrence painted her portrait just before we were married. It's a good likeness."

Before Clarinda could find something suitable to say he got to his feet. "Miss Devereaux, if you wish you may go to your room and rest. Feel welcome to request anything you need. My servants will be glad to attend you."

In response Clarinda also got to her feet and then blurted out, "I hope you are not angry at my using the hair pins."

He looked surprised. "Indeed not. They are of no use to her and they do become you."

Once again she was at a loss of words and he began to limp towards the door. Clarinda made no move to follow him.

"Colonel Pennington, I would dearly like to present you with an explanation of my predicament."

"There really is no need."

"My only reason for staying as close as oak was the fear that you would side with my step-father."

He cast her an ironic look. "I might still do so after your explanation."

"You have proved yourself a just man and I will be content for you to judge for yourself."

"Very well. I shall forgo port and take tea with you in the drawing room."

She tended to walk slowly out of consideration for his injured leg but it suddenly occurred to her that there was no need.

The drawing room had linenfold panelling as did many of the other rooms, lending it a cosy atmosphere. Turkey carpets covered the floor, a fire roared up the chimney and Colonel Pennington ushered her to one of the tapestry chairs which stood near the fireplace.

"You will be warmer here."

She was disconcerted by his thoughtfulness. It was such an unaccustomed luxury.

"Your home is very pleasant," she commented as he sat down, resting his cane against the side of the chair.

"I enjoy living here," he answered. "It's a quiet life but one I have come to covet."

"Then you do not aspire to the *ton*, or to be a Corinthian."

He smiled faintly. "I used to—once. My social life was once quite a hectic one. Now I am content to live my life here, or visit friends and relatives when the mood arises."

She looked down at her clasped hands. "You have an enviable life."

He was gazing at her sombrely. "How odd you should think so. My sister-in-law regards me a pitiable creature."

Clarinda was angry at the thought. "She has no notion of such matters. My stepfather has arranged for me to marry Lord Frampton. *That* is pitiable."

Just then two footmen entered the room bringing with them the china and the tea kettle which they placed on a table between Clarinda and her host.

"Would you?" Colonel Pennington asked after one of the servants had lit the lamp beneath the kettle.

"It would be an honour."

Under his scrutiny she brewed tea and after she had handed him his cup, one of delicate Rockingham china, he said, "So that is why you ran away—this arranged marriage."

"I regard it a good reason."

"To you perhaps but you must be aware that an arranged marriage is by no means uncommon and if every chit ran away from such a situation the countryside would be awash with them."

"I own that it is exceeding common, but the thought of marrying Lord Frampton was more than I could bear."

"I trust you informed Sir Hector of that fact."

"In no uncertain terms," she answered with a sigh.

"Hence the beating."

She lowered her eyes and he asked, "Has that happened before?"

"No, but I feel he would have liked to on occasion in the past. However, it will not happen again, I vow." She looked up at him. "Do you consider me wicked for my refusal to comply with his wishes?"

He put down his empty cup. "Lord Frampton is not a man I would consider a fitting husband for a girl of gentle breeding."

Clarinda felt as though she could have embraced him, but she stifled the desire.

"He is as dissipated as Sir Hector who is as wicked a creature as you are like to meet. Oh, I know you cannot be aware of it, but I am quite persuaded his behaviour hastened my mother's death. My father was a good man. There was nothing to prepare her for Sir Hector's callous behaviour. Now he is in dun territory and a marriage to Lord Frampton is the only way he can gain control of my own fortune."

"Why does he not have control of it now?"

"Under the terms of Papa's will it is only available to my husband or, if I am unwed when I become twenty-one, to me. What a blessing his will was so particular."

"And when do you become mistress of your own affairs?"

"I attain my majority in six months' time."

He looked at first surprised and then abashed. "Earlier today you looked to be a mere child. You are indeed a woman, but I would have thought you far younger." A moment later he asked, "Where were you bound today?"

"To London," she answered, with great relief at the change of subject.

"To relatives?"

She shook her head. "There are none, but I have friends there. Girls with whom I attended an academy."

"Do any of them know you are coming?"

"Unfortunately everything happened so suddenly. There was no time to plan anything or to despatch a note."

"Oh, Miss Devereaux, how foolhardy of you!"

"I had no choice," she answered in outraged tones. "I had to leave before worse ills befell me."

"You might have run from one danger into another just as bad."

She looked away. "So I discovered, but I cannot be sorry I left."

He drew an almost indiscernible sigh. "You cannot remain here."

With her eyes still averted, Clarinda murmured, "I am fully aware of that, sir. I shall leave at first light. You have been indulgent enough and I will not presume upon your kindness any longer than that."

"You mistake my sentiments, Miss Devereaux. Personally you are welcome to remain. Your company is pleasant and I would gladly offer you sanctuary, but it won't do, I'm afraid. It wouldn't be proper, for one thing, but most important is the likelihood of Sir Hector meeting the gypsies on the road. For a guinea or two they will have no compunction in telling him of your meeting, and no doubt he will be able to trace you back here with very little effort."

"I would not have his wrath descend upon *you*, Colonel Pennington. I have been thoughtless."

He smiled and Clarinda thought it a rare occurrence.

"That is not my prime concern, Miss Devereaux. Had you informed me of your intention to join relatives in London I would have sent you on your way with no further ado, but in all conscience I cannot sanction your journey to so uncertain a welcome."

She put her empty cup down on the table in front of her, a trifle irritated by his manner once more. "I assure you, Colonel Pennington, I shall contrive handsomely."

"It is possible, I do not doubt, but mayhap you would allow me to suggest an alternative . . ." He looked at her speculatively. "If you go to London and discover your friends unable or unwilling to help you, you may find yourself exposed to even greater danger than you have already faced. London, Miss Devereaux, is a dangerous place for the unworldly."

"Perchance, that is why Sir Hector is so fond of being there."

A faint smile crossed his lips once more and she added, "Danger lurks everywhere, as I have only just discovered."

"There are dangers you could not possibly imagine for a young woman who is unwise to them. Even if you do find sanctuary you still chance discovery, for Sir Hector is bound to follow the road directly to London."

There seemed to be a distinct chill in the air despite the fire roaring up the chimney and Clarinda shuddered. It seemed there was no sanctuary.

"You are trying to frighten me," she accused a moment later.

"I am merely attempting to show you the error of your ways."

"What am I to do?" she whispered, gazing at him in despair. "I cannot go back."

"I wouldn't dream of allowing you to do so. London is not the only place on earth in which you can find safety. Sir Hector is mostly unlikely to discover you in so unfashionable an abode as Bath."

She sat up straight but as she did so winced, for her body still ached abominably from the beating, and she had walked a long way since setting off from Birchwood. Her ordeal had been greater than she had realised.

"Bath!"

"Your surprise is an indication of its suitability."

"Is that why you suggest it?"

"Partly. My mother lives there with my sister, Beth—at least for part of the year. Beth is to come out next Season, but that need not trouble you. For now it will afford you a place of safety."

She continued to stare at him and he went on, leaning forward slightly. "My mother, I am sure, would be delighted to accommodate you until you are free of all constraint and can live openly again where you choose."

His words went round and round in her mind.

"If you find the notion agreeable I can pen a note to my mother and despatch it first thing in the morning. It will reach her well before you do."

"It sounds a most agreeable plan, but what if she doesn't want a guest in her house?"

He smiled again. "Mama is the kindest person you are ever like to meet, Miss Devereaux. She will welcome you in any event, but if you grant me permission to acquaint her with the facts of the matter you may be certain she will insist upon giving you sanctuary."

"You may certainly tell her. Secrecy was for my own protection, for I could not rely upon anyone's sympathy. It is nothing of which I am ashamed."

"So be it," he said with satisfaction. "I take it you concur with the plan itself."

"I am overwhelmed."

"You have a long journey ahead of you, so I suggest you retire early. I shall pen that note immediately and arrange for it to be despatched. I think it best if you pose as a relative of my mother. She has rather a large number of them and it will not go amiss with anyone."

He took hold of his stick and got to his feet. Clarinda followed suit. Seated, with nothing apparently wrong, he appeared a normal man, and when his features softened, even an attractive one. Whenever she saw him walk her heart was filled with pity, but she knew he was not a man to welcome such a sentiment and she strove to hide it.

"This afternoon whilst you rested it came to me that hiding you in Bath was the ideal solution to this little problem."

"This *afternoon*," she echoed, looking at him in amazement. "But that was *before* Sir Hector arrived and you knew nothing about me or my situation."

He was leaning heavily on his stick but he still towered over her.

"My dear Miss Devereaux, it is patently obvious that young ladies of Quality do not flee their homes for paltry reasons, and it was quite clear to me that you had been sorely abused."

"I do not imagine I am alone in suffering at his hands. Indeed, Sir Hector deserves to be punished for his crimes."

"In the fullness of time I do not doubt that he will."

He walked with her to the door and when they'd reached it she turned impulsively to him once more. "How can I ever thank you for what you're doing?"

"You have no need." His face looked suddenly tense and it was as if his mind was far away. "One day, Miss Devereaux, I might have cause to thank you."

He held open the door and as she crossed the hall towards the staircase those enigmatic words echoed in her mind, but she was truly exhausted by such an eventful day and she soon dismissed them, allowing herself to submit to the luxury of sleep, content in the knowledge that it was safe for her to do so.

Five

They were coming to the end of their journey. Clarinda felt a stirring of excitement; it was as if a new life was beginning, one that could only be better than that which had gone before.

Her mother's untimely death had precluded any real social diversion and, of course, Sir Hector had taken pains to divorce her from any outside activity. It was not in his scheme of things to allow eligible young men access to so fetching and wealthy a girl.

Now this new life opened up before her, be it only for a short while, and the excitement stirred inside her. Bath was not a centre of social importance any longer, but for one so uninitiated in the ways of the *ton* it was enough. She was also aware that after her twenty-first birthday she would be free of that odious man for ever, mistress of her own destiny, with sufficient wealth to allow her to take advantage of that precious freedom—providing Sir Hector did not find her first.

Clarinda shuddered at the very thought. Sitting opposite to her in Colonel Pennington's comfortable travelling chaise Kate looked suddenly concerned for her new mistress.

"Are you cold, ma'am?"

Clarinda shook her head and smiled reassuringly. "No, Kate, I am quite comfortable, I thank you."

The rigours of the journey hadn't troubled her at all after all those hours on the road when she had left Birchwood. Colonel

Pennington's travelling carriage was well-sprung and upholstered with the softest leather. The windows fitted snugly and allowed in no draughts, so this, by comparison, was total luxury.

They had travelled in silence for some time. Kate was not as garrulous as some maidservants. Indeed she appeared quite overawed for most of the time.

When Clarinda at last tired of the view from the carriage window she looked at the girl. "Kate, it was kind of Colonel Pennington to suggest you accompany me, but you must understand that for six months I shall have no money with which to pay you."

The girl's cheeks grew red. "That's all right, ma'am. Colonel Pennington told me himself he'd still be payin' my wages, and if truth were told, I'd not bother about wages for the chance of being a lady's maid. It's a once-in-a-lifetime chance, my mam says. I just hope you'll be pleased enough to keep me on, ma'am."

"I hope I shall be able to, but my future is rather uncertain just now. I can make you no promises."

"Yes, ma'am. I do understand." Her eyes shone with excitement as she glanced out of the carriage window. "I've never been away from Cressfield Manor before, so 'tis quite an adventure for me."

Clarinda looked at her with interest. "Were you born at the Manor?"

"Yes, ma'am. M'dad's a gamekeeper on the estate. Been there man and boy, he has."

Clarinda's interest quickened. "So you've known Colonel Pennington all your life."

"No, ma'am, only since he married poor Mrs. Pennington, who passed on. Cressfield Manor was Mrs. Pennington's house when she was Miss Kent, part of her portion, so I'm told. Mam was poor Mrs. Pennington's nursemaid when she was a babe and then her personal maid. When she passed on Colonel Pennington asked Mam to run the house for him, which she was pleased to do. Didn't want the Manor sold to strangers, you see."

Clarinda looked bleak. "Mrs. Pennington must have been very young when she died."

"Aye, only six months wed, and poor Colonel Pennington away in the Peninsula fighting those horrible Frenchies." Her eyes grew wide. "You don't think Boney'll come here, do you, ma'am?"

Clarinda laughed at such concern. "No, Kate. I believe that danger is over now. The

Russians almost destroyed the French army when it retreated from Moscow last year."

The maid shuddered. "Just as bad, them Russians, so they say. Not civilised at all."

Clarinda laughed again, for no threat was as great to her as that from Sir Hector Liddell.

"I wouldn't know; I have never seen one."

"Lady Pennington has a *black* page," the maid went on, still wide-eyed. "Ain't seen one o' them before."

Once again Clarinda gave the girl her attention as the road began to descend and the town of Bath could be seen huddled in the valley.

"*Lady* Pennington?"

"Not Colonel Pennington's mother. Lady Dulcie Pennington, his sister-in-law. Married to Sir Aubrey, she is. She came to Cressfield Manor once. She's a very fine lady, all condescension, my mam says."

"So Colonel Pennington has an older brother."

Kate nodded vigorously. "Sir Aubrey is a very fine gentleman."

"Colonel Pennington seems to live a very lonely life at Cressfield Manor."

"As like as not it's because he feels closer there to Miss Amelia than anywhere else."

The carriage picked up speed now it no longer had to negotiate the steep hills on the approach to Bath. Clarinda glanced out of the window, admiringly. There were rows of neat town houses which had wrought iron railings at the front of them. Some had elegant carriages waiting outside, with liveried servants holding the horses. To someone as unaccustomed to town life as Clarinda they made a very fine sight.

When the horses began to labour up a steep incline she remarked, "My word, what a hilly place this is."

The carriage negotiated the hill and peering out of the window, Clarinda saw ahead of them an elegant crescent of town houses facing acres of parkland.

"This must be the Royal Crescent where Lady Pennington lives!" she cried. "Kate, I do believe we have arrived at last."

The carriage came to a halt outside one of the houses. Moments later the steps were let down and, gratefully, Clarinda stepped out of the chaise, luxuriating in the opportunity to straighten up. Then she looked around her, inhaling the invigorating air.

Beyond the park, the town of Bath stretched out as far as the hills in the distance.

As the door to the house opened and several servants came out, Clarinda found it rather amusing, for there was no luggage for them to unload save for a cloakbag containing some night apparel which Mrs. Kellett had found for her. From the fineness of it, Clarinda guessed it had once belonged to the dead Amelia Pennington and felt a little strange wearing the garments, but concluded she had no choice, and she was grateful.

A glance in the dressing table at the inn where they had spent the night assured her that the bruises and lacerations were fading, and she no longer looked so hideous. In a few days they would have gone completely, but Clarinda knew she would carry the mental scars of that beating for the rest of her life.

The carriage was moving away and drawing a small sigh she went into the house at last. Just as she entered hesitantly, a small plump lady with iron grey curls covered by a lace cap, came hurrying down the stairs. She stopped halfway down.

"Miss Devereaux?" Her face broke into

a smile of welcome. "My dear, welcome to Bath."

She hurried down the last few stairs as Clarinda pushed her hood from her hair. "Lady Pennington." She looked not the least bit like her tall, lean son. "It's so good of you to have me stay."

Lady Pennington took both Clarinda's hands in her own and Clarinda noticed that her eyes contained a similar warmth which could, on occasion, be seen in her son's.

"Nonsense." She studied Clarinda's face carefully. "If my son is to be believed, this is an errand of mercy."

Inexplicably, Clarinda's eyes filled with tears. "He has been so kind and I fear I invaded his privacy, which he clearly prizes."

"Tush! A lady in distress is just what a gallant man like Brooke needs in his life. He broods alone far too much at Cressfield. I am grateful to you for diverting his mind, my dear.

"Well, do come upstairs to the drawing room and warm yourself by the fire. You must be quite done up after your ride."

"It was quite pleasant."

A footman divested her of what had become a dusty cloak and Clarinda followed Lady Pennington up the stairs.

"Ah, but travelling is so tiring."

"I truly enjoyed it. You see, it is such a novelty to me. It is years since I travelled any distance."

As they went into the drawing room, Lady Pennington cast her a pitying look. "You have been sorely used."

A fire was roaring up the chimney and the room was immediately welcoming. The furniture was exquisite; all the very latest vogue with a faintly Egyptian look to it.

"What a lovely room," Clarinda couldn't help but cry. "Your taste, Lady Pennington, is superb."

"Alas. I cannot take the credit, my dear. My daughter-in-law must be given her due. She brought me Mr. Chippendale's catalogue and all the furniture was ordered direct from it when I purchased the house several years ago. My elder son married you see, and I had no mind to live in his shadow in the dower house. I have always visited Bath in the past for I find the waters beneficial. Living here was a sensible decision I have yet to regret."

She ushered Clarinda to a sofa near the fire, saying as she sat down beside her, her hands folded in her ample lap, "I have sent Beth to buy ribbons in Town, so we can have a coze alone. She is the dearest child but tends to chatter on so." She laughed. "Like her mother, you must be thinking. You may find us too gregarious."

"After years of enforced isolation at Birchwood it can only be welcome, Lady Pennington. Does your daughter know of my predicament?"

The sparkle left Lady Pennington's eyes. "No. I considered it best not to confide in her. You need have no fear that she wouldn't guard a secret, but it is best if as few of us as possible know. It is most unlikely that your step-father will come to hear of your being here, but it is as well for you to pose as my great-niece as Brooke has suggested. I have a great many, you know, and they visit me here from time to time, so on this occasion no one will think it amiss."

"Your daughter might."

Lady Pennington laughed. "Even Beth has lost count of all my many relatives."

"It is kind of you to offer me sanctuary and I hope my staying here doesn't inconvenience you, ma'am."

Lady Pennington put one pudgy hand over Clarinda's. "My dear, what nonsense!

I am quite delighted, you may be sure. This is a welcome diversion for me and may be of benefit to you, too. The good waters of Bath will soon restore both your spirit and your constitution. When Brooke comes to visit he will scarce recognise you."

Clarinda looked at her with interest. "Is Colonel Pennington coming?"

"He has not as yet declared his intention, but I have no doubt that he will. He often visits me and no doubting," she beamed. "he will wish to assure himself that all is well with you."

Suddenly the sound of a commotion in the hall outside diverted her attention and a moment later the door burst open with little ceremony.

"She's here!" a voice cried and then a slightly built girl came rushing into the drawing room, her bonnet askew, a pair of steel-rimmed eye-glasses perched on the end of her nose. "Oh, oh dear, I do beg your pardon, Mama."

Lady Pennington smiled and said, not unkindly, "You must try not to act the hoyden, my dear. It really is not becoming in one your age. Now," she went on with scarce a breath. "This is Clarinda Devereaux. My daughter, Beth."

The girl flushed. "Oh, it is so good to have you here." Then she looked accusingly at her mother. "Mama, she is not at all like Cousin Eliza. Moreover I must declare she is too pretty to be a part of our family. *Quelle surprise!*"

Clarinda looked away in confusion at the mention of the family connection as Lady Pennington replied, "I cannot imagine why she should favour Cousin Eliza. Now, Beth, Clarinda has only just arrived and she is very tired. Be a dear and show her to her room, but try not to be such a prattle-box, at least until she has had an opportunity to rest."

"I cannot help my excitement. I am as gay as a goose in a gutter." As Clarinda got to her feet she confided, "After all, it's so good having a *young* person here. Everyone in Bath, I must warn you, is so old."

"She means everyone who is over five and twenty," her mother pointed out indulgently.

As Clarinda followed Beth out of the room she noticed that the girl carried a substantial armful of books. At Clarinda's questioning look Beth became suddenly abashed.

"Mama sent me for ribbons for my new bonnet, but I could not resist a browse around the circulating library in Milsom Street. It is next but one to the mercer's shop. Do you read, Clarinda?"

"Sometimes."

"Mama says if I read any more than I do at present I shall turn into a blue-stocking and frighten off all my suitors, but as I don't have any it hardly matters. Even if I did, I wouldn't care what they thought. I adore novels in particular although I am not averse to a volume of poetry. Mrs. Radclyffe and Scott are my favourites, and needless to say Lord Byron's poetry is quite sublime. You really should read them. Such romance and adventure! It is so much better than real life."

Clarinda longed to tell her she had endured sufficient real life adventure for a long time to come, and romance would have to wait until she was free of Sir Hector's guardianship, but Beth was now gazing curiously at Clarinda's welter of fading bruises.

"Your face is all done up. How on earth did you manage to hurt yourself so badly?"

For a moment she was taken aback and then replied breathlessly, "I fell from a horse."

Beth looked appalled, which did not ease Clarinda's conscience one iota. "I am horribly frightened of those awful beasts, so you do not surprise me at all. You might have been disfigured permanently, like my brother, Brooke. Do you know him?"

"We have met," Clarinda answered guardedly.

The girl's face took on a dreamy look. "Do you not think he is splendidly romantic?"

At this Clarinda could not help but retort, "I think such a disability is a great pity."

"Oh yes, indeed," his sister agreed in a breathless voice. "The leg is a dreadful burden for one so active, but he rarely allows it to inconvenience him, I assure you." She smiled again. "But I would like to think my husband might mourn *me* as he does poor Amelia.

"Oh dear, Mama will give me one of her set downs if I prattle on any more. Please forgive me, Clarinda. I know you must be quite done up and longing to rest."

Clarinda smiled. "There is nothing to forgive."

Beth's plain face beamed again. "Oh, how I wish I were pretty like you." She went towards the door. "I just know it's going to be fun having you here, Clarinda."

After she had gone Clarinda continued to

smile, but when she looked around the simply furnished room to the pitifully few belongings Kate had been able to put out on the bed, she wondered what Beth would make of so small a collection of clothes.

Six

As it turned out she had no cause to concern herself about her lack of possessions. Long before dinner was served Lady Pennington herself came to Clarinda's room carrying a number of gowns over her arm.

"Now, I know these are not in the forefront of fashion for this Season, but I am persuaded they will do handsomely."

Clarinda eyed them in amazement. If they were not of the current vogue that fact was not immediately evident to her. Lady Pennington had brought her a selection of gowns for both day and evening; satins, velvets as well as lightweight muslin.

"Lady Pennington!" she gasped. "They are quite divine. They must have cost a fortune. You must not on any account spend the blunt on me in this way. I could not countenance it."

The lady laughed. "My dear, they have

cost me nothing. On her last visit to Bath my daughter-in-law left them in my keeping rather than take them home with her. She had purchased so many new ones whilst she was here there really was no room for these in her boxes."

Clarinda began to look bewildered. "Will she not be angry if I wear them when she wishes to have them back?"

The elderly lady laughed again. "Indeed she will not. Lady Dulcie wears only the very latest of fashion. A gown six months old may just as well be ten years out of date. Foolish, I grant you, but young ladies are always the same. I recall that I was, too, many years ago."

"I would be honoured to wear them. They're quite exquisite. I have never seen such workmanship."

"Her build is somewhat similar to your own, but if any alteration is necessary I don't doubt your maid will be able to accomplish it quite easily. She seems a sensible sort of a girl."

"She is a treasure, which is something I owe entirely to Colonel Pennington with whom she is in service. My maid at Birchwood was on familiar terms with my step-father, and I always felt she had been installed to spy on me."

"You poor dear," crooned Lady Pennington and then, sighing, she added, "I shall send your maid up to you to help you with the gowns. There are all manner of garments still in store, not to mention bonnets and gloves. We shall have so much fun altering them for your use. Naturally though, when you are come into your inheritance, you will be able to buy gowns of the finest stuff."

Clarinda laughed, unable to envisage the time when that would come to be. "Lady Pennington, I shall never require anything finer than these."

"Ah," her hostess replied, "but you have not as yet had the opportunity of visiting the emporiums in Bond Street."

Just as she was about to leave the room, Clarinda said, "I do feel guilty about telling Banbury Tales to Beth. She is so sweet."

"My dear, I do applaud your frank nature, but I fear she is a tattle-basket. Her tongue is so unguarded at times, I am afraid of her indiscretion, although I do know she would not betray you deliberately."

"But will she not wonder at my lack of

belongings and even not knowing of such a relative before now?"

Lady Pennington chuckled. "My dear, I really do believe I could write some of those novels Beth for ever puts her nose into. I told her you were the daughter of one of my nieces who married against the family's wishes and hasn't been spoken of for years. Now your parents are dead and you are in straitened circumstances. I believe that does cover everything quite neatly."

She looked delighted with her own inventiveness and Clarinda began to laugh. "Oh, Lady Pennington, you really are quite wonderful."

"Thank you, dear," she answered demurely before going out of the room, to leave Clarinda to examine the gowns more closely and with great delight.

In the weeks which followed her arrival, Clarinda found herself growing more and more fond of Lady Pennington and her daughter. They seemed to set themselves out to be kind to her and their continual chatter was welcomingly diverting.

Once the bruises had faded entirely, Lady Pennington insisted that Clarinda accompany her and Beth to the Baths to be dipped and, afterwards, to take the waters in the Pump Room to the accompaniment of music and general conversation.

At first Clarinda was reluctant to be seen outside the house in Royal Crescent, for fear of being recognised, but Lady Pennington quickly persuaded her that the risk was a very small one, and in any event she could scarcely spend the next few months hiding inside the house.

"Do you really think your step-father will look for you *here?*"

Clarinda shook her head. "London and Brighton certainly, but not Bath," she agreed.

"Indeed not. He has no reason to think you here. Only old-fashioned widows are to be found in Bath nowadays. When Beau Nash was alive, ah, that was quite a different matter. Nowadays it is a genteel kind of society, and a dull one."

"It cannot be dull if you are here, Lady Pennington," she responded.

"Dear child," the widow murmured.

And so Clarinda did make an appearance at the Pump Room. She was at first quite naturally tense but the assembled visitors accepted her gladly as a kinswoman of Lady

Pennington and as such she was invited to accompany her wherever she went.

After their first few visits to the Pump Room, Clarinda accompanied Lady Pennington and her daughter to various functions, both public and private. A breakfast was held at the Sydney Hotel, a card party at the Upper Assembly Rooms, a rout at one lady's home, and a drum at another. They even attended a production of *The Perfect Wife* at the Theatre Royal. Clarinda also discovered the joys of the emporiums in Milsom Street at which she happily window-shopped as Beth waited impatiently to visit the circulating library.

"Our social life has certainly improved since you arrived," Beth told her one day as she peered out of the drawing room window at the rain which slanted across it.

Clarinda had been busily embroidering a fire screen as a gift for Lady Pennington when she looked up in some surprise. "Did you not socialize before, Beth?"

"Not nearly as much as we do now. A new face always stimulates interest. Bath is so small. It is bound to be so. Oh, this dreadful rain. How I long to go out."

"I am told you will be going to London for your Season before long."

"It is an age yet; months away. In any event, I do not think I much care for the prospect."

Clarinda put down her needlework. "Why ever not? I am told a Season is the highlight of any girl's life."

Beth turned her back on the depressing scene outside and faced the other girl. "Just look at me. I am no beauty, Clarinda. I shall be outshone at every turn, and pray do not laugh at me. 'Tis important."

"I would not laugh at you for anything," Clarinda replied truthfully. "But I am persuaded that once you are come out you will enjoy the Season hugely."

"I shall be obliged to sit out every set at every ball and at Almack's—if I contrive to procure a voucher which is doubtful. The aim is for me to find a husband, but which suitor would fall in love with me?"

Clarinda smiled. "Dearest Beth, you have the sweetest disposition. You cannot fail to attract devotion."

"Oh, that is of no account. And I have no notion to be wed for my portion which is the fate of many, I have heard."

Of this Clarinda was only too well aware. She was not well-pleased to be reminded of the fact.

However, realising that Beth was truly unhappy about her situation, she put her head on one side and considered her friend properly for the first time.

"Your hair curls naturally and is very pretty, Beth. You could cut it short in the latest mode which I am persuaded would be an improvement. Kate, my maid, is very clever with her hands. I am persuaded she could do it for you if you wished."

The girl continued to look doubtful as she fingered her hair. "I can do nothing about my eye-glasses. I can see so little without them."

"Then they will have to remain. It is of no consequence. When you are in London you will be able to buy new gowns and bonnets, and be all the crack. I'm persuaded you have no need to trouble your head, Beth dear."

"It is easy for you to say so. You have already attracted a good deal of attention since you arrived. You cannot help but do so."

"You surely exaggerate."

"The fact that Lord Tetbury continually fawns upon you and is always to be found at your side cannot be deemed an exaggeration."

Clarinda was startled as Beth went on with scarce a pause, "Mama hopes to see you settled before you leave here. She regards it as her duty to her family in a way. I am bound to say, on this occasion, she will not find it a difficult task."

At this Clarinda laughed. "Oh Beth, I am sure you are mistaken. I have not thought of it nor has Lady Pennington spoken of it to me. After all, I am come merely to take the waters."

"I am persuaded Mama will have thought of it; she thinks of little else. You must recall, Clarinda, you are almost one and twenty. Dulcie, my sister-in-law, is no older than you and yet she has three children in her nursery."

Clarinda's face grew red and as a diversion she picked up her needlework once again.

Beth wandered across the room, toying idly with the spinet as she passed. "Do you not consider that Lord Tetbury has quite tolerable features, Clarinda?"

Once again Clarinda paused in her sewing and then drew a sigh. So that was it; Lord Tetbury. She recalled now that the personable young viscount invariably contrived to be at the Pump Room when they attended, and often he was to be found at the Circulating Library, too.

"Yes, indeed, he is quite tolerable," she replied at last, stabbing her needle into the canvas.

"He is heir to the Earl of Melton. It is said he has an income of twenty thousand guineas a year." When Clarinda did not comment she went on a moment later, "From all I have observed of late he seems exceeding fond of you. I am sure you must have noted it."

"You mistake his good breeding and manners; that is all which makes you believe he has formed an attachment."

Suddenly Beth stamped her foot. "Clarinda, you are being most provoking." Her friend stared wide-eyed at her. "You are being less than frank with me in this matter."

Once again Clarinda put down her sewing. "Indeed I am not. I have only met Lord Tetbury in your company on brief occasions. Any civility he has displayed was always towards us both and your mama."

"I do not believe that. It is you he seeks to favour and you must be sensible of that. Any woman would be."

"I cannot make you believe me, Beth, but

I do take exception to being accused of telling untruths."

As soon as she had spoken Clarinda realised that in some instances a liar was precisely what she was, and she bit her lip. At the same time, Beth, full of contrition, came hurrying across the room. She sat down beside Clarinda on the sofa and clasped her hands in hers.

"Oh, dearest Clarinda, I beg your forgiveness. How could I be so churlish? If you wish not to tell me your inner feelings you must not. I have no right to ask it of you."

Embarrassed Clarinda replied, "There is nothing to reveal. Lord Tetbury is merely a pleasant young man whom I have met whilst abroad with you and Lady Pennington."

Beth looked away. "I am a chucklehead to plague you so. Mama often says I am as mad as May butter, and I fear it is so."

She got up and walked back towards the window, peering out mournfully. "If only this wretched rain would stop we could walk in the Fields."

"It will be exceeding muddy for some time to come."

Suddenly Beth stood on tip-toe to get a

better view of the street below. "Clarinda! Clarinda! Oh, do come and see. Can you guess who is walking along the Crescent?"

For some unaccountable reason Clarinda's heart began to beat fast and her mouth became dry.

"Who?" she asked in a small voice.

"Lord Tetbury! He is walking along the Crescent at a brisk pace. He looks most handsome in his greatcoat." She gasped. "Do you think . . . ? Oh yes, he's going to call in here. What do you suppose he wants?" she asked as she turned on her heel, looking wide-eyed at her friend.

"More to the point, shall we receive him, Beth?"

"Yes, indeed."

A few minutes later when the viscount was ushered into the drawing room Clarinda was busily embroidering and Beth was sitting demurely in a chair, a book open on her lap.

"How kind of you to call, Lord Tetbury," Beth said immediately he had entered the room.

"I was passing," he replied, none too convincingly, "and deemed it proper to pay my respects."

"Please be seated," Beth invited, a faint flush tinging her cheeks.

As he brought forward a chair, Clarinda had the opportunity of scrutinising him properly for the first time. She supposed his features were quite presentable, but the sight of him did nothing to disturb her composure even though the knowledge of his regard could not help but flatter her.

As he sat down he cleared his throat. "You did not take the waters this morning . . ."

"The weather . . ." Clarinda explained.

"Quite so. It has been atrocious. When I met Lady Pennington in town earlier she assured me all was well with you both and suggested I call in—if I happened to be in the area, which by good fortune I am."

"How fortunate it is for us that you are," Beth beamed.

"The morning up until your arrival has been quite wearing."

He smiled uncertainly, glancing at frequent intervals at Clarinda. Now she had been made aware of his attitude she couldn't help but wish he would not show such partiality—at least not towards her. His favourable countenance and twenty thousand a year did nothing to move her.

A few moments' silence ensued before Clarinda said, "Does the rain show no sign of slackening, Lord Tetbury?"

"A little," he responded.

"Do you . . . ?"

Just as Beth ventured to speak the viscount said, addressing himself to Clarinda, "I wanted to make quite certain both you ladies will be attending the subscription ball at the Upper Assembly Rooms on Friday."

"Yes, indeed," Beth enthused. "Such an event is not to be missed and we would not dream of doing so."

The young man seemed satisfied and, finding his tongue more easily now, asked, "I hope you, Miss Devereaux, are enjoying your stay in Bath and benefiting from the waters."

"Oh indeed. The waters are conducive to my health and Lady Pennington is an exceptional hostess. My stay couldn't be more happy."

He flushed with pleasure. "Such a declaration indicates that you will be staying a while longer."

Beth looked vexed and Clarinda was more than ever sorry Lord Tetbury tended to address himself to her.

"I shall be remaining at least until August. Lady Pennington and Miss Pennington will, after that, be departing for London. Miss Pennington is to make her debut next Season."

He looked suddenly anxious. "And you, Miss Devereaux? Do you not go with them?"

She drew a small sigh. "My plans are at present uncertain, my lord."

He flushed deep red. "You must deem me impertinent to examine you so closely."

"By no means, my lord. It is a sign of your interest."

Beth got up and wandered restlessly across to the window. Clarinda could think of no way in which to bring her into the conversation.

Suddenly Beth gasped. Clarinda could hear a carriage and horses on the cobbles outside and wondered who Beth had seen this time.

Then, quite unexpectedly she laughed. "La! We have another visitor." Both Clarinda and the viscount looked at her with polite interest. "If it isn't Lady Carlton. She will be miffed that Brooke is not here."

Immediately she had spoken Lord Tetbury got to his feet. "Then I shall take my leave of you for now."

Beth turned on her heel, looking dismayed. "I assure you Lady Carlton's arrival does not mean you must go, my lord."

He smiled faintly. "I did not think so, but I do have several more calls to make. Pray excuse me."

He bowed stiffly to them both and although Clarinda was somewhat relieved to see him go her friend merely stared in dismay at the door for a long time after he had gone.

Seven

After a few moments had elapsed Beth rounded on Clarinda. "Now do you see what I mean? You cannot mistake his partiality."

"I can only hope you are mistaken. I have done nothing to encourage his attentions. Now, enough of Lord Tetbury; *who* is Lady Carlton?"

Beth smiled impishly and Clarinda was glad to see a return of her good humor. "She is a youngish widow. Quite wealthy, too, I understand. She is not often in Bath but I am quite persuaded she wishes to marry

Brooke. Mama will not hold that it is so, but you cannot convince *me* it is not."

Clarinda laughed. "I fear you see matches for all of us."

"Tis merely that I am unblinkered."

A footman announced the arrival of Lady Carlton who swept into the room, her huge feathered bonnet almost as wide as the doorway.

Clarinda was startled to see how handsome she was, and so imposing a character.

"Dear Beth!" she cried as she entered. "How fine you look and so grown up, too. I cannot credit it!"

"Lady Carlton, we did not hear that you were in Bath."

"I have only today arrived, and determined, upon orders of Colonel Pennington, to convey his felicitations to his relatives."

"Brooke?" Beth asked.

"I have lately seen him in London."

Beth started forward eagerly. "Oh, do give us news of him, my lady!"

"All in good time," the countess replied, smiling slightly.

She seated herself on the sofa, removed her stockinette gloves and stared unashamedly at Clarinda who felt quite abashed by her scrutiny.

"Allow me to present my kinswoman," Beth said quickly, "Clarinda Devereaux."

"Devereaux," the countess repeated. "That is a name I have heard of late. I seem to know it."

Alarmed, Clarinda did not know what to say, but, looking mischievous, Beth added, "Of the Northumberland Devereaux."

"Ah yes, indeed, and yet I am persuaded I have heard the name somewhere quite recently, I am sure. I shall recall where and when, have no fear."

Quickly, Clarinda said, in an attempt to divert her thoughts, "I trust your journey was congenial, Lady Carlton."

The countess waved her hand in the air in a languid gesture. "My dear, what journey is?"

She took a jewelled snuff box from her reticule and inhaled a pinch.

"Is there some pressing reason for your visit?" Beth ventured.

Lady Carlton looked at her. "Does there need to be?"

"'Tis only that the London Season is still in progress."

Lady Carlton sat back against the cushions of the sofa, smiling wearily. "I am all done up, my dear, and need to take the waters. How quickly they restore my spirit." Her eyes narrowed wickedly. "I noted young Tetbury leaving here as I arrived. Now, which one of you girls does he favour?"

Clarinda would have preferred not to return to that topic but, downcast, Beth answered, "He came to see Clarinda."

"He came to see us both!" the other girl retorted.

"You are being too modest, my dear, by far," the countess crooned. "One can scarce blame the young man. After all, you are uncommonly fetching."

Clarinda blushed. "You are much too kind, Lady Carlton."

"Tush. 'Tis only the truth. Tell me, Miss . . . er . . . Devereaux, have you come out?"

"No, my lady. Family circumstances denied me the opportunity."

The admission caused the countess to regard Clarinda with rather more interest than before, but before she could continue to question her, Beth ventured eagerly: "Did you not mention that you had seen my brother in London?"

There was little doubt of the girl's devotion to her brother and it warmed Clarinda's heart.

The woman's face was transformed by a look of delight. "Indeed, I did. It was a great pleasure to see him and in such good heart, too. He was looking in finer feather than I have ever noted before, and was obliged to tell him so."

"'Tis not like Brooke to mix in tonnish circles these days."

"Exactly so!" Lady Carlton's eyes were bright with excitement. "I am persuaded he is no longer moping so dreadfully. After all, none of us can resurrect the dead and poor Amelia . . . Well, enough said of such matters."

"If only Brooke would come to Bath," Beth complained in a woebegone voice.

Clarinda realised she would like that, too. It would be good to see him again.

"Ah yes, indeed." Lady Carlton gathered up her gloves and got to her feet. "Unfortunately, this needs must be only a fleeting visit. We shall no doubt meet again before too long a time." She laughed. "In Bath how can we not? Give my felicitations to Lady Pennington and convey my regrets at not seeing her."

"We will," Beth vowed.

As the door closed, the room seemed bereft of her overpowering presence. Beth let out a long breath.

"La! What a woman."

"She is a fine lady, and seemed . . . nice."

"Don't let her fool you, Clarinda. She is forceful. I am persuaded she wishes to marry Brooke, and if that is her intention I am afraid he has little chance of escape."

"You sound disapproving."

"Can you imagine my brother married to *her?*"

"I . . . don't know," Clarinda mused, pondering on the thought.

Beth laughed. "Then you cannot know Brooke."

Clarinda had to admit that was so.

They did not catch sight of Lady Carlton for several days, and for some reason Clarinda was not sorry. The woman's declaration she had heard her name recently was far from reassuring. She had almost, but not quite, managed to put the thought of Sir Hector from her mind, but she was always aware that her step-father would be frantically seeking to find her whilst she remained under age.

After a while she confided her fears in

Lady Pennington who seemed not the least perturbed by them.

"You must not allow her to plague you, my dear, for her prattling is of no account."

"I cannot help but speculate on where she heard mention of my name. Sir Hector will have been seeking news of me in all the salons."

"I don't doubt it, but let me tell you, Lydia Carlton, before she married the earl, was on the verge of being unacceptable in polite society. Her marriage made her respectable at last, but she still seeks to claim a knowledge and the acquaintanceship of elevated families which simply does not exist."

Clarinda's mind was thus set a little at rest. However, there was no respite from the ubiquitous Lord Tetbury who contrived to be present wherever they happened to be. Pathetically, instead of being vexed at his marked partiality to Clarinda, Beth was glad enough of the opportunity to see him so often. Her natural garrulity was immediately stilled in his presence and Lord Tetbury, being no conversationalist himself, left Clarinda to hold court, thereby, perhaps, giving the viscount the notion that she returned his regard. It was becoming a ridiculous situation, but one out of which Clarinda could see no easy way.

"If Lord Tetbury does not ask me to stand up with him at the ball on Friday," Beth declared as they returned to the house from the Pump Room one day, "I shall die wearing the willow."

"What humbug," her mother retorted.

"Oh, I am quite persuaded he will ask," Clarinda broke in quickly. "He cannot fail to do so after seeking such a close acquaintanceship of late."

"He will most certainly ask *you*," came the retort.

"Really, Beth, I am quite surprised at you," her mother blandished. "You are usually so level-headed, so full of good sense."

"Love makes fools of us all," she answered darkly.

"You are not yet come out," Lady Pennington reminded her. "There will be all manner of eligible and handsome young men in London who will contrive to make Lord Tetbury look a clodpole."

"I don't doubt that the Town is awash with handsome young men, but they will not look at me more than once."

"What a buffle-head you are," Clarinda

scolded, much to the girl's alarm. "I should not have such an opinion of myself."

"You do not need to."

"If I were dissatisfied with some aspect of my appearance, I should do my utmost to alter it."

"There!" Lady Pennington exclaimed. "It is Clarinda who is full of good sense."

Beth looked so crestfallen Clarinda leaned forward to squeeze her hand. "You will fall in love many times yet; you will see."

"How can you know? Have you ever been in love?"

Feeling oddly uneasy about that question Clarinda was forced to look away. "No, but surely one uncaring beau cannot signify the end of the world."

"I look forward to the day when you discover that it is." Suddenly, as the carriage crested the hill and came into the Royal Crescent Beth's demeanour underwent a dramatic change. "Mama! Only see the carriage standing in front of our house!"

Although Clarinda could not envisage Lady Carlton creating such delight in Beth, nevertheless she dreaded to see her again.

Lady Pennington turned to obey her daughter's direction and then her demeanour also brightened. "Brooke! That is Brooke's carriage. How splendid!"

"What a delightful surprise," Clarinda agreed, and then with less certainty, "I trust it is a surprise."

"Had we known he was coming do you not think we would have said something?" Beth asked, laughing delightedly. "My brother is wont to call unexpectedly and I cannot take him to task for it."

The girl sat back in the squabs, smiling foolishly. "Come to take the waters indeed!" The other two ladies looked at her and she went on, "Lady Carlton. I am all done up!" she cried in a reasonable facsimile of that lady's voice. "Brooke will have to guard his tongue in future or she will shadow his every move."

Clarinda grinned and Lady Pennington said scoldingly, "Has it not occurred to you that your brother may wish her to be here with him?"

"Oh, never," Beth declared. "He couldn't possibly be such a buffle-head."

The carriage drew up with a jerk behind the other one. As soon as the steps were let down Lady Pennington hurried into the house to greet her son. The two girls followed rather more sedately and just as Beth was about to go inside, too, Clarinda held her back.

Beth looked at her curiously as she said in a hesitant manner, "About Lord Tetbury..."

Beth's face relaxed. "Pray don't let my megrims trouble your head. I am quite sensible that it is none of your doing. You have never so much as flirted with him, and if I did so I still couldn't make him favour me."

"But if I were not here..."

"It would make no odds, you may be certain."

"If you wish me to go, I will, Beth. I have not sought Lord Tetbury's regard and I most certainly have no desire to hurt you."

Beth's eyes grew wide. "Oh no, you must vow you will not go. Please, Clarinda!"

It was the other girl's turn to relax. "I am relieved to hear you say so."

"No more than I. Moreover, if Lord Tetbury declares himself and you wish to accept I will be the first to wish you happy."

Clarinda's eyes opened wide and she laughed, "Beth, there is no chance of that. I am not in love with Lord Tetbury."

Beth looked sad then, which surprised her. "What a waste."

She turned and went quickly indoors.

Rather more slowly Clarinda followed. Colonel Pennington was in the doorway of the hall, taller than she recalled and, she realised, he appeared to be more relaxed. Beth pitched herself headlong into his arms.

"Brooke, you deserve a set down," she declared. "You've stayed away from us for far too long."

"Perhaps, but you and Mama are always welcome to come to Cressfield Manor whenever you wish."

"You know how Mama dislikes travelling."

"Therefore I must swallow my dislike of it to come to you." He held her away, gazing at her. "You are becoming quite a woman, Beth Pennington."

"But not woman enough," she answered, suddenly despondent again.

His eyes strayed across the hall to where Clarinda was standing shyly in the doorway. His smile rekindled and he limped towards her with Beth still clinging to his arm.

"Miss Devereaux, how well you look."

"And you, Colonel Pennington," she answered pertly.

"She has improved vastly since she arrived," Beth pointed out.

"'Tis obvious to me that Bath water

agrees with you. There must be something in Mama's praise of it."

She blushed and Beth went on. "She also has an admirer."

"Dozens of them I shouldn't wonder," Brooke Pennington responded, and Clarinda's blush grew deeper beneath his close scrutiny.

"You cannot criticise," Beth scolded and when he looked at her in amazement she went on, "You may well look askance, Brooke Pennington, but I dare say it's no surprise to you to learn that Lady Carlton is in Bath. You must have told her you were coming."

He laughed at her outrage. "I may well have done so, goosecap, but Lady Carlton has every right to visit Bath, too. It is not our exclusive preserve, my dear."

Beth cast him a look of disgust. "And you are not Lady Carlton's."

Just at that moment Lady Pennington came bustling in, straightening her cap as she did so.

"Now, my dear, I assume you are lodging again at North Parade."

She was breathless, no doubt from issuing frantic instructions to the servants and out of excitement.

"My man is there now arranging our apartments."

"Then you will stay and dine with us tonight."

"Not tonight, Mama. I have too much to do."

"Tomorrow then?"

"With pleasure. Aside from the delight of your company, I long to hear all your news."

"*You* have been in London," she retorted with a laugh.

"Tattle, I find, is the more intimate in Bath. We always know the victim."

She laughed delightedly and he went on, "Now I have paid my respects, I must take my leave of you for the moment." He glanced at Clarinda who still remained by the door, apart from the others. "It is good to see you again, Miss Devereaux."

Her cheeks grew pink and as he was about to pass her on his way out she asked impulsively, "Shall you be coming to the subscription ball on Friday night?"

He hesitated for a moment before answering in a thoughtful tone, "Dancing is not one of my best pursuits nowadays, Miss Devereaux."

She felt like biting off her tongue, but

Beth saved her some embarrassment by saying, "Tush, Brooke. You are not obliged to stand up in the sets. There will be other diversions. Do come. It would please us greatly to see you there."

He cast her an indulgent smile, something which, Clarinda guessed, no one but she could have elicited from him. "How can I resist such a plea? The prospect of escorting no less than three beautiful ladies is too much of a pleasure to forgo."

Beth giggled before saying, "Your tongue is well hung nowadays. It was never used to be."

"Yes, it was," their mother contradicted, giving him a speculative look.

In the hall he accepted his beaver and gloves from the footman. As he left he raised his hat to them. "Until the morrow, ladies."

Clarinda remained where she was until she heard his carriage leave. Then Beth gave a little squeal of delight.

"Mama, he is almost like his old self again."

Lady Pennington still looked thoughtful. "So it would appear, but I cannot help but wonder what has put him in such high snuff."

"Oh, what does it signify?" Beth cried.

"He is in good heart and I can only rejoice in the knowledge. And is it not splendid to have him here with us again?"

Clarinda did not reply but quietly reflected that it was rather nice.

Eight

Brooke Pennington glanced at his gold hunter before returning it to his pocket. "I wonder where Beth can be?"

He was standing in front of the fireplace in his mother's drawing room. Lady Pennington and Clarinda were sitting nearby, clad in their finest gowns, Lady Pennington with a number of feathers in her hair.

"It is quite unlike her to be late for dinner," Lady Pennington remarked. "Her appetite is always so hearty."

"She may be ill," her son suggested.

"I think not," Clarinda broke in quickly. "I was with her not two hours ago and she was in excellent spirits."

"A headache often afflicts one quite suddenly," Lady Pennington mused. "There was a time, I recall, when Beth suffered them frequently."

"I think," Clarinda said with a smile,

"that the delay is due entirely to Beth's wish to look her best at the ball tonight. You see, my maid is so clever I lent her to Beth, but Kate was obliged first to attend me."

"That would certainly account for her lateness," Lady Pennington agreed. "Perchance, Clarinda, my dear, you would be kind enough to enquire of her how long she is like to be."

She hastened to do Lady Pennington's bidding, aware that Brooke's eyes were upon her as she crossed the room. He might well be marvelling at the change in her. On their first meeting her face had been almost unrecognisable and clad in an outdated habit and dusty cloak she must have presented a most disreputable appearance.

Now, clad in one of Lady Dulcie's discarded gowns of peach-coloured crepe de chine, embroidered with seed pearls, Clarinda knew she looked quite different, but his critical scrutiny disconcerted her nevertheless.

With rather red cheeks she hurried up the stairs and knocked on Beth's door.

"Beth, 'tis I, Clarinda. Your Mama and Colonel Pennington are waiting to go in to dinner."

"Oh dear, am I very late?" came a faint reply.

"Late enough to cause concern. Is anything amiss?"

"No, nothing, I assure you. Pray tell them I shall be only a few moments longer."

"May I come in?"

"Oh, I beg of you do not!" came the startling reply. "I will be down presently."

Considerably taken aback, Clarinda snatched her hand from the door knob and stepped back a pace before turning on her heel and skipping back down the stairs.

"Beth is not ill," Clarinda was able to report when she returned to the drawing room.

Lady Pennington and her son had been engaged in earnest conversation and the way it ceased abruptly when she entered served to tell her she had interrupted something private. Lady Pennington looked rather pale and concerned and her son uncharacteristically discomfited.

"She is finishing her toilette," she added lamely.

"In that event," the lady replied, getting on her feet, "we shall go in to dinner now. We cannot tolerate these delays. What can the child be thinking of?"

Clarinda hurried to fetch Lady Pennington's shawl and fan which she had left on the sofa. "I believe it is only because she wishes to look her best this evening."

As they passed in the hall Colonel Pennington said in a low voice, "Miss Devereaux, I am persuaded that gown becomes you far more than it ever did my sister-in-law."

Colour flamed in her cheeks and she scarcely knew where to look or indeed how to respond to such a compliment. She was aware that he was not a man to voice useless flummery. A compliment—or indeed a criticism—would never be given lightly and, therefore, was all the more valuable for that.

"Beth!" Lady Pennington cried, thus saving Clarinda's embarrassment, or the need to reply.

All three of them looked up as Beth stood on the stairway, awaiting their reaction, which was a startled one. The person standing there was well-nigh unrecognisable.

Her gown of white satin and crystal beads was the most beautiful Clarinda had ever seen, but it was Beth herself who made them gasp.

She had allowed Kate to crop her brown

locks into a short and very fashionable style of angelic curls which framed her face most flatteringly. She had dusted her face with powder and there was also a trace of rouge on her lips, giving her usually colourless features a touch of vibrancy.

"My God!" her brother exclaimed. "What a beauty! Who can she be? Will no one tell me?"

"Don't be such a chuckle-head," Beth replied, thus shattering the illusion with her normal tone. "I shall never be a beauty whatever I do."

"I beg to differ. You are quite breathtaking, I assure you. If only I could bespeak every dance with you I would be the happiest of men."

"It is just as well you can't; standing up with my brother for every set is no achievement."

He bowed slightly, saying in an ironic tone, "Why, thank you, my dear, but do heed your careless tongue; such flattery is like to turn my head."

Clarinda chuckled and Lady Pennington confided in a low voice, "How delighted I am to see her making an effort, Clarinda. I despaired of her ever being anything but a dowd."

"'Tis amazing the miracles love can perform," she whispered in reply.

Lady Pennington responded with a curious look before returning her attention to her daughter. "Beth, do come down now, dear. You have delayed us an unconscionable time. Cook will be furious if dinner is allowed to grow cold."

"Tush! Who cares what Cook thinks?"

"Well, I do," her mother retorted. "Good cooks are not easy to find, and Mrs. Convers is anxious to acquire ours."

"Come along down," Brooke told her. "I would like to take you in to dinner, *if* a mere brother may be accorded that honour."

Beth dimpled with pleasure but a moment later it was evident why she delayed; without her eye-glasses she was unable to see well and she began to feel her way down the stairs with obvious difficulty.

The three watchers in the hall below stared at her in dismay as she clung to the stair rail and felt with her foot for each step.

Clarinda was the first to ask, "Beth, where are your eye-glasses?"

"In my room, of course. It would entirely spoil my appearance if I was obliged to wear them tonight."

"But, Beth, you must wear them. You cannot see clearly without them."

"That is too bad. I cannot wear them tonight."

"How will you recognise your acquaintances?" her brother enquired.

"Mama can lend me her quizzing-glass, which will suffice."

"But, Beth . . ." her mother protested.

She almost missed the last stair and would have fallen if her brother had not caught and steadied her. "Don't be a chucklehead," he scolded. "Do as Miss Devereaux asks."

" 'Tis no use," Beth said in despair. "No effort of mine can change anything."

Clarinda put her arm around the girl's shoulders. "That isn't so, dearest. You look truly lovely tonight. Wearing eye-glasses cannot change that."

"Flummery. I am just as I ever was."

"Indeed I hope you are—just as good-natured and as full of good sense. Heaven forbid you should change in those respects."

Her eyes met those of Brooke Pennington who smiled and suddenly Clarinda felt much lighter of heart. She moved away from

Beth saying, "Let me go and fetch your eyeglasses for you."

As she started up the stairs Brooke said, "I am not at all certain the invalids of Bath will be able to withstand the onslaught of two such glamorous ladies tonight."

Beth began to laugh and as she ran up the stairs Clarinda cast him a happy smile. The unhappiness and terror of the past seemed far away.

Nine

Carriages choked the streets around the Upper Assembly Rooms. Although its situation was not far from Lady Pennington's house in Royal Crescent, it took them some time to reach it, for functions at the newer of the Assembly Rooms were always popular, more so nowadays than those at Simpson's rooms closer to the town centre.

Chandeliers blazed with countless candles and as they entered Clarinda felt a stirring of excitement at the prospect of attending her first ball, even though it was a public one. She had heard of the dazzling social occasions at the Pantheon in Oxford Street, London and in Almack's exclusive preserves. Even more fantastic were the private balls of the *ton* at Devonshire House and Holland House. Each function vied for greater splendour than the one which had gone before.

However, Clarinda could not be more enthusiastic if she had been invited to one of them. She had already made the acquaintance of many of those present, and, accompanied by Colonel Pennington, who looked quite handsome in his dark blue evening coat and satin breeches, she could not help but feel proud. He always dressed with care, she noticed, and yet there was nothing of the dandy about him. The pristine whiteness of his neckcloth and the precise way it was folded would have done justice to that prime arbiter of fashion, Beau Brummel himself.

"Can you see Lord Tetbury?" Beth asked, as soon as they joined the milling crowds inside the ballroom.

"No, but I have no fear that he will soon make himself known."

Beth snapped her fan shut. "Oh, indeed he will. I trust you feel able to stand up to every set with him."

Clarinda chuckled at her sarcasm. "He would not be so foolish as to ask."

Beth's improved appearance was attracting a good deal of surprised attention, Clarinda noted with satisfaction. Almost as soon as they arrived Lady Pennington was claimed by one of her cronies and borne away for a rubber of whist.

"That is Mama engaged for the evening," her daughter commented, a mite tartly.

"Each to his own pleasures, my dear," her brother replied.

"And what shall yours be?"

"I shall renew acquaintances and marvel at the energy expended in the dancing."

"You talk like an old man," Beth scolded. "You are but two and thirty."

Colonel Pennington smiled indulgently. "And is that not *very* old, my dear?"

Beth tapped his arm with her fan. "Faddle. You are always roasting me."

"There are certainly sufficient partners for you ladies," he declared after he had glanced around the crowded room.

It suddenly occurred to Clarinda that he was behaving like a surrogate father and the notion irked.

"Would that we could stand up with you," she replied.

He smiled faintly. "It would be my honour, ma'am, I assure you."

Once again Clarinda felt disconcerted and then Beth nudged her quite viciously. "Here comes Lady Carlton. How opportune!"

True enough, the countess was bearing down on them. Her ample bosom was squeezed tightly into a green velvet evening gown which did not quite succeed in containing it entirely. A profusion of matching green feathers was festooned in her hair and they seemed to sway precariously as she moved.

"Brooke! How delightful to see you here." She glanced at the girls who curtseyed before returning her delighted gaze to the colonel. "How remiss of you not to call on me."

"My apologies, ma'am, but I arrived only a short time ago and have been engaged since in family affairs."

"Well, I trust they are now resolved and we may have the honour of your company. You do intend to stay in Bath, I trust?"

"A little while at least."

She smiled with satisfaction before transferring her attention to the two girls again. "How charming you both look tonight."

"Thank you, my lady," Clarinda replied

to cover Beth's churlish silence. "It is quite delightful for me to be here."

The countess threw back her head and laughed heartily. "How charming it is to find someone who is delighted at this rustic gathering. Do you not think so, Pennington?"

"I find such freshness charming."

Clarinda's cheeks flushed, uncertain whether or not he, too, was indulging in ridicule. She realised she did not mind if it came from Lady Carlton, but from Colonel Pennington, it cut her to the bone.

Nevertheless Clarinda persisted. "Do you not think Miss Pennington looks particularly fetching tonight?"

"Oh, indeed. There is a great improvement, I own. What a pity, though, you are obliged to wear those eyeglasses. They are such a blemish."

She linked her arm into his. "Come, Pennington. These girls will contrive very well on their own and I wish to have a long-overdue coze with you. It is an age since we last met."

"'Tis no more than a se'nnight," he protested laughingly, to which she replied, "Well, I own it seems like a month!"

Colonel Pennington inclined his head to

the girls and was led away by Lady Carlton who, it seemed, never stopped talking. Beth let out an exasperated sigh.

"Can you imagine *her* as a sister-in-law?"

"No," was Clarinda's unequivocal reply as she, too, watched them disappear into the heart of the crowd. "However, I am persuaded she truly means well; she is merely tactless."

"You are, as always, exceeding generous, but you are not like to have her as your sister-in-law. Brooke is nothing to you." Clarinda looked away in dismay as, heedless, Beth went on, "It is sufficient that my other brother's wife is overbearing and condescending to an extreme. Two of them would be outside of enough, although I dare say meetings between the two would be most interesting."

Clarinda laughed and then asked in a more serious tone, "Beth, what was Amelia like?"

The girl was scanning the crowds for sight of Lord Tetbury. An elderly gentleman paused to engage Clarinda in a minuet and when he had gone Beth returned her attention to her friend.

"Oh, poor Amelia. Why do you want to know?"

Glancing around Clarinda shrugged her shoulders slightly. "I am vaguely curious about her, that is all."

"She was perfectly sweet. Everyone loved her."

"How did she die?"

"Smallpox."

"Oh, that is indeed dreadful."

"Yes, indeed it was. Poor Brooke was returned to his regiment in the Peninsula when she became ill. Everyone thought she was making a good recovery but, oh, Clarinda, she was hideously marked. One day she contrived to find a mirror which everyone had been hiding from her, and from that day began a decline, which I have always declared to be poor-spirited of her."

Clarinda looked at her friend in astonishment. "Because she died?"

"Willed herself to death more like, because of her face. I can understand it, naturally, but I still deem it faint-hearted if she considered Brooke would love her the less."

In the wake of Clarinda's shocked silence Beth went on, "Mama is convinced that Brooke's heroism at Vimeiro was merely a way of expelling his despair at the news which would have reached him by then. We are persuaded he never intended to survive."

Her words hung in the air for a moment or two. Clarinda was profoundly affected, her mood at odds with the gaiety in the room and the sound of the musicians who had begun to play for the opening set.

"Oh, my goodness. He's here!"

Thoughts of the tragic Amelia Pennington fled from Clarinda's mind as she turned round to see Lord Tetbury coming towards them.

"Miss Devereaux." He bowed. "May I bespeak the honour of standing up with you for the cotillion?"

"By all means, my lord."

Beth had shrunk away to hide behind her fan, but Clarinda drew her forward, saying pointedly, "Miss Pennington and I are both so enjoying the evening."

His eyes opened wider then. "Miss Pennington, ma'am, I didn't re . . ." Glancing round he said quickly, "I was not immediately aware of your presence."

Beth smiled coquettishly. "I am so easily overlooked, my lord. You must not feel embarrassed."

Nevertheless he continued to look uneasy until at last he said, "If you are not already engaged, perchance you would do me the honour of standing up for this country dance."

Beth was evidently taken aback and it was Clarinda who answered, "I don't believe she is engaged, my lord."

As Beth went off clinging to Lord Tetbury's arm she turned to give her friend a bewildered smile. Sighing with satisfaction Clarinda wandered around the room in search of acquaintances and was soon claimed for the set herself. Afterwards more gentlemen bespoke dances and there was hardly a moment when she was not partnered.

As she whirled around the floor she caught sight of Colonel Pennington from time to time, and he was always within Lady Carlton's grasp. Clarinda was beginning to dislike the woman as heartily as Beth did, even though it was an ungracious feeling. Lady Carlton had never been anything but civil to her, but as a wife she would not suit Colonel Pennington at all, Clarinda decided.

"Miss Devereaux."

She turned on her heel at the sound of Brooke Pennington's voice. She was breathless from the dancing and enjoying herself hugely. Her eyes sparkled and her cheeks were flushed with colour.

"Is this not the most delightful ball?" she asked as she caught her breath.

"Evidently," he replied, gazing at her indulgently. "May I bespeak the honour of taking you in to supper? It is the one thing I can do as well as other men."

Clarinda's bright countenance faded slightly. "I would be honoured to be escorted by a hero of Vimeiro," she answered.

"I am no hero, ma'am."

"That is not the general opinion," she told him as they went towards the supper room. "And I do wish you would not demean yourself, sir."

He looked down at her, a smile playing about the corners of his lips. "Do you seek to castigate me, ma'am?"

"Indeed, I do. I am persuaded that there are few enough pursuits in which you do not excel, and you cannot tell me it is not so."

"I cannot stand up in a dance set with a fetching chit."

Her cheeks grew slightly pink. "That is a mere bagatelle, so why trouble even to mention it? It is of no real importance."

"Dancing is usually important to most ladies I have met."

"It is enjoyable, I own, but not of the greatest import."

"Then I stand corrected."

The supper table was all but groaning with a delightful array of dishes. As she and Brooke made their choice she noted that Lady Carlton was casting them an arch look from across the room, and as a consequence Clarinda held up her head the higher.

When they were seated with their heaped plates she caught sight of Beth whose cheeks were unusually flushed, although that may well have been due to the fact her escort was Lord Tetbury.

Clarinda couldn't help but chuckle at the sight of them, which caused Colonel Pennington to cast her a curious look.

"Lord Tetbury has taken Beth in to supper," she confided.

"Vincent Tetbury is a likeable young man. I have known him and his family for years."

"I don't suppose I am revealing any secrets when I say your sister has thrown her cap over the windmill."

He looked astounded. "Young Tetbury?" She nodded. "But I thought it was you he admired."

"At present he does, but I am earnest in the desire that he will transfer that admiration to your sister who is more receptive to him."

He was concentrating on his feet. "Although I tend to look upon her as a child, I am bound to own that she is growing up fast."

"Indeed she is, and she will make some lucky man an excellent wife."

He looked at her askance. "You are remarkably complaisant about Lord Tetbury."

"I have a high regard for him, of course, but I feel no romantic attachment."

He continued to regard her for a moment or two before saying in a thoughtful tone, "You must know my mother would like to see you settled, as there is no one else to look out for your interests."

His admission drew a sigh from her and she put down her fork. "Over these few months I have been here it has been easy for me to forget my true situation."

"I did not seek to distress you, Miss Devereaux, but I feel some mention must be made."

"You are quite right to do so. I must certainly look to my future before long. Here in Bath it has been so easy to slip into the role of Lady Pennington's kinswoman. Sir Hector has not existed for me for a long while."

"You have had a necessary respite." After a moment's pause he went on, "I do not often venture to London these days, but felt I must to ascertain what, if any, action Liddell was taking."

Clarinda looked at him, her eyes wide with fear. "I do not suppose he has forgotten my existence."

He smiled faintly. "I regret to say not. He is still in pursuit of you. Indeed, he has never ceased to search."

She looked away. "You do not surprise me, Colonel Pennington. He will never give up, even when I am one and twenty. One day he will exact retribution because I cheated him of a fortune."

Unexpectedly he put one hand over hers. "Clarinda, you are perfectly safe whilst you remain within my protection. I would never allow him to harm or put you under any duress."

His declaration caused tears to spring to

her eyes. "I am already indebted to you far more than I could ever repay."

"You must not think so."

"But ultimately it will be to no avail. Sir Hector will never give up, nor will he ever forgive me."

"Take heart, Miss Devereaux; you will soon be past your birthday."

"That will make no odds, I fear." Her voice was husky with emotion. "Throughout my stay here, although I have sought not to think about it, I have always known I could not escape his wrath for ever, and my worse fear is that he should discover that you have aided me. He is a ruthless man and his vengeance will envelop us all."

"I assure you that I, too, am a man to be reckoned with."

She smiled at him then. "I do not doubt it, but you are also an honourable man—he most certainly is not. Even if time enough passes and perchance I marry, I fear he will wreak his vengeance on those who are dearest to me. Am I to hide for ever?"

He cast her a mocking glance. "Miss Devereaux, I fear you have been reading some of those novels which my sister loves so dearly."

Her cheeks flamed again, this time because of his ridicule. "Now you are roasting me."

"Please forgive me," he said, and seemed truly contrite. "I am fully aware of Sir Hector's true nature, but I must reiterate that you have nothing to fear. Promise me that you will not trouble your head any further on this matter."

After a moment's hesitation she nodded and then she noted Lady Carlton was coming toward them, accompanied by a couple of dandies who had been shadowing her devotedly all evening.

Clarinda suspected that Colonel Pennington drew in a sigh of exasperation, but she could not be certain. Her only certainty was her own fear which he had done little to still, despite his declaration. It was plain that she could not remain under his protection for ever, and if Sir Hector caught up with her at any time, there was little he could physically do, in any event, to prevent him acting just as he wished.

As these uncomfortable thoughts went around in her head Brooke got to his feet and bowed stiffly to the countess whilst Clarinda stood up and curtseyed. She was irritated that Lady Carlton had allowed him to get up; it would have been more thoughtful for her to have indicated he was to remain seated, but on second consideration she knew he would not appreciate that kind of treatment.

"It has been a tolerable supper for such a place as this," the countess commented in a condescending manner which immediately irritated Clarinda.

"We have enjoyed it," Colonel Pennington replied, glancing at the subdued Clarinda in a rather worried manner.

"But your plates are still quite full," she pointed out.

"There is too much."

Lady Carlton transferred her attention to Clarinda who felt not the least like engaging in polite conversation with this woman.

"'Tis evident you are much in demand, Miss Devereaux. Such attention is like to turn a young girl's head."

"I am having a tolerable time," Clarinda answered politely, wishing desperately that she would go away.

"You have scarce been obliged to sit out one set."

"I am flattered you have noticed."

"One can hardly be unaware. In a rustic gathering such as this there is so little of a diverting nature. However . . ."

Colonel Pennington, having finished his wine, put down his glass and said quickly, "I have no doubt, my lady, you will wish to return to London as soon as you are able to contrive."

"Indeed," she answered. "You and I, Pennington, are quite out of place here."

"Not I," he answered, casting her an amused look. "I am something of a rustic myself these days."

For a moment the countess appeared disconcerted but then she addressed herself to Clarinda once more. "Dear Miss Devereaux, I have been endeavouring to recall just where I have heard your name, but the occasion still eludes me."

At the reminder Clarinda started and was glad when Colonel Pennington said in a deprecating voice, "It was I who spoke of Miss Devereaux when we were in London."

"Oh, I am persuaded you did not."

He eyed her with amusement. "Despite your declaration of devotion, I fear you do not even attend my words, my lady."

She looked vexed for a moment before she asked, "Is that what you truly believe?"

"It would seem so."

"Perchance words are merely superfluous

in some circumstances. Pray excuse us. I am engaged for the first set after supper."

Both Clarinda and Colonel Pennington watched her go and when she was out of hearing he said, "I fear Sir Hector shouted your name loud and clear in the hope of discovering someone who knew of you and your whereabouts."

"When she recalls . . ."

"Let us hope she does not."

"And if she does?"

"We will face that situation when and if it occurs. She is bound to come to me first, in any event, and I will ensure her prudence."

Clarinda looked up at him. "There are times when it would almost be a relief for him to find me."

He frowned. "You cannot mean it."

She sighed and then smiled. "No, I do not. I would not for anything bring his wrath down on you and your family."

"Then do as I say; put such a notion from your head. All will end well, I assure you."

She smiled at him again, putting her hand on his. "You do wonders for my spirits, Colonel Pennington."

"Which is just as well, as I recall it was I who depressed them with my talk of your step-father. However, at this moment the orchestra is playing and your *beaux* anxiously await you to partner them."

As he escorted her through to the ballroom where Lord Tetbury awaited to stand up for the cotillion with her she could not help but wish that her partner was Brooke Pennington himself.

Ten

His presence in Bath seemed to elevate the spirits of those living in Royal Crescent. Lady Pennington was in a constant fidge and Beth's mood of despondency had lifted. Her cropped hair had made her aware of her charms and she became more confident as a woman.

"You will be well prepared for your Season," Clarinda told her one morning as they travelled to the Pump Room for the obligatory stroll and glass of water.

"I am hugely looking forward to it."

It was Lady Pennington who answered whilst her daughter stared out of the windows as the carriage entered The Circus and moved smartly towards Gay Street.

"I would as lief stay here in Bath," she answered at last.

"I cannot conceive that you mean it," Clarinda told her in shocked tones. "An opportunity of a Season in London is not to be missed."

"If the object is for me to find a husband, it is of no consequence, for I have already given my heart."

"What humbug," her mother retorted.

"You will see that I am resolved," Beth hissed in dramatic tones. "I will not be coerced into accepting any other, even if it means remaining an old maid to the end of my days."

Clarinda stifled a laugh behind her glove and Lady Pennington's only remark was, "Tush."

The carriage entered the Abbey Churchyard which was crowded with sedan and Bath chairs which transported invalids to and from the baths beneath the colonnade built to protect them from the worst excesses of the weather.

The three ladies disembarked at the Pump Room where a great many people were already assembled. Lady Pennington hurried away to the bath itself where she was regularly dipped whilst the girls went into the Pump Room to enjoy the more social aspect of the ritual.

Several acquaintances stopped to speak and all the while Clarinda was aware that Beth was restlessly seeking sight of Lord Tetbury. No one could miss Lady Carlton's entrance, splendidly attired as she was. She also paused in the doorway, apparently unaware of the disapproving frown of Beau Nash's portrait which hung in pride of place in the Pump Room. Delightful as she found the spa, Clarinda could not help but wish she had lived at the time when Beau Nash was the uncrowned king of Bath, when all the great names of the *ton* gathered there.

Lady Carlton moved around the gathering rather like a queen bestowing her largesse.

Beth watched her, scarce hiding her hostility, but Clarinda could not help but admire her sophistication and style. At Lady Carlton's side she could only feel like a rustic.

"Does Lady Carlton know about Amelia?" Clarinda asked at last.

"I dare say she knows Brooke is a widower," Beth answered carelessly. "What does that signify?"

"Only that if she knows of Colonel Pennington's devotion to the memory of his late wife I wonder she tries to bring him up to scratch at all."

"That is the last thing which would dismay a woman like that. I am only afraid she will succeed." She frowned. "'Tis odd, for I have long since felt that Brooke would marry again if presented with the proper female."

"Oh, and who would you deem the proper female?"

Beth's cheeks grew pink at her friend's teasing. "I wouldn't presume to say, but I do know that Lady Carlton is not his style. Oh dear, Clarinda, I fear she is approaching us."

Sure enough the countess smiled at them magnanimously as she turned from exchanging a few words with some acquaintances nearby.

"Good morning, ladies."

Both curtseyed with due deference to her rank, albeit reluctantly.

"How is dear Lady Pennington? Not indisposed, I trust?"

"Mama is being dipped," Beth replied. "I dare say she will join us here presently."

"And did not you two girls wish to join her? You both look a trifle hag-ridden this morning, I do declare, and after all, life is tedious enough, is it not? Bath is not the most stimulating of towns."

Irritated, Clarinda could not help but say, in a pleasant enough voice though, "Your dislike of Bath is for ever apparent, Lady Carlton. I only wonder that you condescend to stay. It is a trifle dowdy for a lady of your elevation, as I'm persuaded everyone would agree."

The woman's smile faded at so pithy a comment. "There is but one reason for my being here; the waters do wonders for my constitution. There is no denying that." She glanced around, her mood becoming bland once more. "It is so satisfying seeing all these military men around. I do so love a uniform."

Unthinkingly Clarinda said, "My step-father was in the army."

Immediately she had spoken she knew she had made an error. One of Lady Carlton's eyebrows rose.

"Your step-father, dear? Perchance he and I are acquainted. I know so many of our gallant fighting men."

Clarinda laughed. "It is most unlikely, my lady, for he was of no social import."

"Was?"

Clarinda smiled at the sudden thought. "He died—some time ago."

Beth said, "Oh, poor Clarinda; I didn't know."

"From Miss Devereaux's tone of voice I doubt if she cares," the countess commented.

"Alas, that is so," Clarinda replied demurely, feeling on safer ground now. "You are astute indeed, ma'am."

"So it is oft said." Then, looking at Beth, "I do not see Colonel Pennington here today."

Clarinda drew a sigh of relief at the change of subject. It was fortunate that the countess was interested in little beyond her own sphere.

"That is because he is not here," Beth replied, relishing the task.

Lady Carlton frowned slightly. "How odd that is. I was quite certain he would be. Last night . . ." She smiled then in an embarrassed manner. "On our last meeting Colonel Pennington intimated a visit to the Pump Room today."

With an inclination of her head she moved away. Beth let out an exasperated sigh but Clarinda merely watched her every movement until she could no longer be seen because of the crowds. Somewhere inside was a hard knot. Last night. Brooke Pennington had been with the countess last night. He had dined at Royal Crescent and left at a late hour, so there was no doubt it had been a nocturnal visit.

Clarinda was bitterly disappointed in him although she really couldn't say why. There was no reason to suppose he had lived the life of a monk since the death of his wife and Lady Carlton was an exceedingly fetching woman even to someone as biased as Clarinda.

Beth, unaware of her friend's dismay, squeezed her hand before moving away to get closer to Lord Tetbury who had arrived at last.

"Ladies, good morning!"

He at least was in good spirits, Clarinda was glad to see.

"You have little cause to take the waters," Beth retorted shyly.

"No, indeed; that was not my purpose in coming."

"Oh, no?" Beth answered.

The viscount's smile encompassed them both. "I wished for congenial company and I have certainly found it."

Clarinda was scarcely aware of his words,

for Colonel Pennington had just entered the room and she was unprepared for the jab of pleasure which she experienced at that moment. All her dismay at Lady Carlton's revelation suddenly disappeared.

As he gazed around the room, almost unthinkingly she moved away from the other two and raised her hand to attract his attention. When he caught sight of her she was rewarded with a smile and a moment later he laboriously made his way towards her.

"You have only just missed Lady Carlton," she greeted him, the moment they were close enough to speak.

"What a pity," he replied with no real expression.

"I believe she was out of countenance for you had intimated to her that you would be here."

His eyes held a sparkle of mischief. "If that is what Lady Carlton says then it must indeed be so, and here I am. What a crush this is." He glanced at his sister, deep in conversation with Lord Tetbury. "You are being exceedingly tactful, Miss Devereaux."

She chuckled. "If I am it is only because I wished to converse with *you*."

He looked taken aback at her admission. "On any particular topic?"

"Need there be one? Conversation in general can be most enjoyable. Indeed it is a popular pastime in this town."

He laughed wryly. "Oh, Miss Devereaux, do not, I beg of you, become a tattle-basket."

She looked hurt at his response. "If you would rather not . . ."

As she began to move away he caught her by the wrist and drew her back towards him. "I am only gammoning you, so don't get into a pucker. Your conversation, be assured, is always delightful and invariably of great interest, too."

Her cheeks coloured, but she could not deny the renewal of pleasure she felt at his words. So many strange emotions had afflicted her of late, she was truly mystified by her own attitude.

He looked suddenly more serious. "Miss Devereaux, you must be well aware of the passage of time. Soon you will come of age."

"Yes," she answered breathlessly, her eyes downcast. "What shall I do then, I wonder?"

"Do not imagine you will be cast adrift on the sea of life."

Clarinda looked at him. "I would be most obliged if you would do me the service of granting me your counsel."

"As much as I am able, you may be sure. In the first instance you must take whatever steps you can to secure your own fortune."

"How do you suggest I do that, Colonel Pennington?"

She looked at him earnestly and he glanced away from her. "There is time yet, but I would suggest you travel to London with Mama and Beth. You will have passed your birthday at that time. Do you know which lawyer your father employed when he drew up his will?"

Clarinda frowned for a moment and then her brow cleared. "Yes, I believe I do. A Mr. Wellman of Temple Bar. I have heard Mama speak of him."

He smiled. "Good. That is an important obstacle overcome. You must consult with him as soon as your birthday has passed. There will be no difficulty. I am persuaded your late father made his instructions perfectly clear."

She looked suddenly afraid. "It is all very well my travelling with Lady Pennington, but you must not forget that in all likelihood my step-father will be in London, too."

His face grew stiff. "Mayhap he will not be at that precise time. Do not let the thought dismay you. London is a large town, in any event."

"I could not be content, knowing he may turn a corner at the very time I walk along a street."

He gave her a considering look before saying, "It is possible circumstances may change between then and now."

"If only that were so," she murmured in heartfelt tones, "but I cannot envisage how."

He glanced at his sister and said more brightly then, "It is time we interrupted this *tête à tête*."

Responding in a like manner, her dark thoughts cast from her mind once again, Clarinda gave him a disapproving look. "Only a brother could behave in so heartless a manner."

He was already moving towards them. "Then you should be heartily thankful that you do not possess one."

"Colonel Pennington, if I had one like you, it is like I should not be in this morass."

He paused to glance at her again. "Then

you must consider me that brother, Miss Devereaux."

For some reason that notion did not please her as much as it should have done. Whilst she was wondering why, Brooke was addressing himself to the young viscount.

"Good day to you, Tetbury."

The young man beamed good-naturedly. "Ah, Pennington; good to see you."

"I trust my sister is not making a cake of herself."

Beth gasped indignantly and Lord Tetbury became rather red of face. "Her conversation is charming, sir."

Beth looked at him askance. "You are tardy indeed, Brooke. Now you will be obliged to break your heart because you have missed sight of no less a personage than Lady Carlton."

"So Miss Devereaux has informed me," he answered, displaying a good deal of amusement. "Well, I have always regarded punctuality as a virtue, and now I am faced with the consequences of being late."

Beth laughed and put one hand on his arm. "Dearest Brooke, you were always a great funster. It is good to see it in you again."

"If Lord Tetbury will forgive my presumption, may I invite you and Miss Devereaux to ride with me this afternoon?"

Clarinda gasped with pleasure but Beth looked taken aback. "Oh, I cannot."

"Cannot or will not?" her brother demanded, his eyes sparkling with mischief. "Can it be your horsemanship still leaves a great deal to be desired despite my careful coaching?"

"You are heartless, Brooke. It just happens that I have a task to perform which just will not wait."

Clarinda looked at her with interest. "You did not speak of it to me earlier when we discussed the plans for today."

Beth bit her lip. "It was something which occurred quite unexpectedly."

Her brother looked at the viscount and fixed him with a steely look. "Tetbury, I trust this has nothing to do with you. Clandestine meetings will be found out in the end."

Lord Tetbury's face grew red and he began to stammer. "Indeed not, Colonel Pennington. How could you think . . ."

At this Brooke began to laugh to the young man's further dismay and it was Beth who said in a disgusted tone, "You must not mind my brother, my lord. He has an abominable sense of humour which is a trial to us all."

"You commended it only moments ago," her brother retorted, laughing all the more.

Lord Tetbury relaxed and smiled faintly, although Clarinda was not convinced he appreciated Colonel Pennington's sense of humour.

Beth suddenly looked mischievous. "Of course, there is no reason why Clarinda may not go with you this afternoon."

Clarinda became immediately flustered. "No, there really is no . . ."

"Of course she may," Brooke mocked. "Why should Miss Devereaux miss such a delight if you are not sensible of it?" He turned to Clarinda before she could protest any further. "Horse or carriage? The choice shall be entirely in your hands."

She flushed with pleasure. "Horse, I think. It is an age since I was in the saddle."

"So it shall be. Ah, here comes Mama. No doubt she will whisk you off to important tasks in Milsom Street. Heaven forbid I should delay you."

Lady Pennington looked much improved by her dip in the Bath, or perhaps it was because she had sight of her son. Clarinda could understand her pleasure; she was looking forward to the ride he had promised with no small enthusiasm.

Eleven

The sun continued to shine and, dressed in her own riding habit which had been cleaned and pressed since her arrival, Clarinda waited patiently that afternoon for Brooke Pennington's arrival.

Beth, playing patience, looked up at her. "My brother is invariably punctual, so you may be certain he will be here at the appointed hour. It just isn't time yet."

Clarinda came away from the window, ashamed of displaying such impatience.

"I mistook the time," she said lamely and was cast an ironic look by her friend. "Where *are* you going this afternoon?" she asked suddenly, "Or is it that Radclyffe streak in you which has engineered this ride with your brother?"

Beth gave her an artless look. "Why should I do such a thing, Clarinda? Shame on you for such thoughts." She looked suddenly uneasy. "Forgive me, but I cannot say."

Clarinda sat down next to her on the sofa.

"It is not an assignation after all, is it, Beth?"

"Brooke was jesting this morning; you are not." She looked at her. "No, it is not an assignation. I have no need of one; I can see Lord Tetbury whenever I wish. I cannot say, but I promise you it has Mama's blessing and you *will* discover what I am about in due course."

"Well, I shall be obliged to be content with that, shall I not?"

Beth gave her an impish grin. The longcase clock in the corner chimed the hour and as the last chime died away the sound of hooves on the cobbles outside could be clearly heard.

Instantly, Clarinda was on her feet once more and making her way to the door. "Oh heavens, here he is," she cried as she glanced in the mirror on her way out, adjusting the tilt of her hat.

"I cannot conceive why you are in such a taking!" Beth said artlessly. "After all, 'tis only my brother."

As the door slammed shut behind Clarinda, Beth began to chuckle and then went to fetch her own bonnet and pelisse, humming happily to herself all the while.

The horses had only just stopped outside

the house when Clarinda came out. Brooke looked surprised and she realised she was behaving in a hoydenish manner which was not entirely becoming to a lady.

"Punctual, Miss Devereaux," he declared. "What an admirable—almost unique—trait in a lady."

Aware that he was teasing her she immediately became more demure and allowed the groom to hand her up into the saddle.

"I trust my invitation has not disrupted your important social life," he said as she settled into the saddle and there was more than a hint of irony in his voice.

"Far from it. This is a welcome diversion, Colonel Pennington."

"Indeed. I can well imagine why. Shopping and perambulating about the Pump Room can take on the semblance of monotony after a while."

She cast him an acid smile, not certain how she should take his gentle teasing. "You mistake my sentiments, sir. Such pursuits, to me, could never grow tiring, especially when in the company of Beth and Lady Pennington."

"I am obliged to them for sparing you this afternoon."

"Lady Pennington is engaged in a rubber of whist," she told him as they set off.

"I should be surprised and worried if she were not. Do you think you could ever become accustomed to such matronly pursuits, Miss Devereaux?"

"I dare say I should. I am not a high-flyer as you may have observed."

"Ah, but I'm persuaded that is only because you have not yet been afforded the opportunity."

"Given it, I would remain as conventional as I am at present, I assure you."

"Conventional is not a word I should apply to you."

She cast him a quick glance. "You are roasting me, Colonel Pennington."

"Indeed I am not!" he protested, but not very convincingly, and then a few moments later, "I am glad to afford you the opportunity of sitting in the saddle. Beth has no liking for it at all. If there is any future for her with Tetbury she will be obliged to learn to enjoy it, for he owns some of the best cattle I have ever seen."

Clarinda laughed. "Then I don't doubt she will. I was always more used to riding my horse astride at Birchwood, but I dare say doing so here would be deemed outrageous."

"You would cause a sensation."

She glanced at him again. "Do you have any plans to go up to London?"

"I shall certainly be there when Beth makes her debut."

"Her heart is already engaged, but a Season in London is not to be missed. My mother had one and spoke of it to me."

"What a pity you could not have one, too."

Clarinda smiled sadly. "Even if my mother had lived, I fear Sir Hector would have contrived to have me wed to a man of his choice—Season or no Season, but I should have liked to have mixed with the *ton*, and perchance meet the Prince of Wales. Or perhaps I should call him the Prince Regent, for that is what he is now."

Again he laughed. "He would undoubtedly find you enchanting, but you would be disappointed in him." When she gave him a curious look he went on, "Prinny is a sad figure of a man nowadays, I fear, consoling himself with elderly ladies of the Court."

Eager for information, she asked, "Have you actually met him?"

"Several times during my career, but not

in recent years. I am bound to own I have always found him to possess a deal of charm."

"And Brummel?" she asked. "Do you know Brummel?"

He laughed then. "Everyone knows *of* him, but I cannot be numbered as one of his cronies. I fear my leg makes it impossible for me to wear clothes with the degree of perfection Mr. Brummel demands, so I cannot be counted amongst his friends."

Clarinda was outraged. They were riding through the town and Colonel Pennington raised his beaver to acquaintances whom they passed on the way. It seemed that the sunshine had brought everyone out for a stroll.

"What impudence! You look as fine as any man I have ever seen."

When he cast her an intent look she became abashed and looked away in confusion.

"The talk of the Town, when I was there," he went on and she was sure it was to cover her confusion, "was the rift between Brummel and the Prince. No doubt you have heard of it."

She was able to give him her attention again. "I have the opportunity to hear little gossip from Town. At Birchwood I was quite remote from all else, save from *The Gazette* from which I could glean a little news whenever my step-father was at home."

"Well, I can assure you it is so. I am afraid insults have been exchanged which bodes ill, for even one so influential as Brummel cannot insult his future King with impunity."

"I am amazed that he dares."

"Unfortunately, over the past few years that gentleman has come to believe everything he says and does is sacred. We must blame those sycophants who constantly flatter and fawn upon him."

When Clarinda looked at him it was with shining eyes. "Oh, it must be quite wonderful mixing with such people. Byron, for instance. Beth cannot wait to meet him when she goes to London; 'tis the only reason for any small enthusiasm on her part. We have both read *Childe Harold's Pilgrimage*, which I cannot in all truth find remarkable, although she does. Have you also met Lord Byron, Colonel Pennington?"

"We have been guests at the same gatherings, but he is invited less and less. He, too, is less popular of late. At present he is the subject of some unpleasant tattle, and although outrageous behaviour amongst our class is not out of the ordinary, one must take care not to outrage one's peers."

"I should never dare!"

They had left the Town and taken one of the narrow roads into the hills. The summer air was pleasantly warm, the birds twittered all around them in the trees and hedge-rows which were alive with a bright tapestry of wild flowers.

It was difficult for Clarinda to believe that she had been there for months; it seemed so short a time since she arrived. Her very enjoyment of her time there made the weeks go faster, she was sure.

When they came to the brow of a hill, Brooke slowed his horse and said, "This is a good place for us to rest the horses for a while."

She dismounted before he did, saying, "Colonel Pennington, may I help you?"

Immediately, Clarinda knew she had made an error, for his face grew red. "No, I thank you," he said sharply, and she drew back.

Surely enough he dismounted with no trouble, snatching his stick from a slot in the saddle. Then he fixed her with an angry stare that almost made her tremble.

"The day I require a lady to help me dismount, I shall forgo the pleasure of riding."

As he limped away from her, her eyes filled with tears of regret and frustration. They were at a vantage point from which the whole of the town could be seen in its splendour. However, it was blurred to Clarinda, who had eyes for only him at that moment.

After a few moments of indecision she hurried up to where he was standing with his back towards her. "Oh, Colonel Pennington, Brooke, I have wounded you and I am so sorry. I would as lief bite off my tongue as wound you."

He looked at her then and she was glad to see all that anger gone from his face. "And I am too sensitive by far. You meant well."

"I am a chuckle-head, and I beg of you to forgive me."

For a moment he did not reply and then after gazing at her for what seemed to be an age, he said with a sigh, "Who am I to forgive you?"

Her eyes were wide, questioning him silently. He turned away from her once more and she said, "I don't . . . understand."

He smiled, waving his cane in the direction of the town. "A pleasant vista, is it not?"

She applied herself to it. "Oh yes, indeed."

Immediately though her attention returned to his proud profile. She wished she could find something to say to him, to ease the hurt she had unwittingly caused, despite his easy forgiveness. His mood was suddenly a strange one and not easy to understand.

Tentatively she put one hand on his arm. "Brooke . . ."

He looked down at her again and whatever she was about to say was forgotten in that long moment when her eyes met his. It was a moment full of discovery and her myriad feelings were explained at last. It was as if a great mystery had been revealed and all Beth's agonies were now clear to her. She was also in love.

Abruptly he stepped back, away from her importuning hand, and then with slow deliberation walked away from her. Once again she watched him, her heart full of secret longings.

He went directly to her mount and when she realised he was waiting for her, she hurried to him.

No word passed between them as he handed her up into the saddle. If she had caused him offence now, when she had discovered her love for him, it would be too cruel.

As they cantered down the lane he said, as if nothing had passed between them, "Miss Devereaux, I have been remiss in not telling you news of your horse, Mungo. He is in fine spirits at Cressfield Manor, you will be relieved to know."

She was more relieved than he could ever discern, mainly because his tone was quite normal again.

"I did not doubt it, Colonel Pennington. I left him in good hands. My own mare, Bess, of whom I am exceedingly fond, is at Birchwood. The day I left I had ridden her hard and therefore was obliged to leave her behind in favour of a fresh horse."

"Shall you ever go back?"

"It is doubtful. Whatever transpires, Birchwood is the property of Sir Hector Liddell. Papa left it to my mother, you see."

"He could scarce envisage a disastrous

second marriage, but it is as well he entailed your own inheritance."

"Sir Hector may yet gain control of it."

Brooke Pennington smiled faintly. "I think not, my dear."

They had entered the town once more. To Clarinda's mind the ride had scarce been the pleasant canter she had envisaged, even though it had started out that way. However, she could never regret it, for the secret of her heart had been revealed at last. She stole a glance at him, wondering at her own feelings which were so new they almost alarmed her.

Someone called out to him and he acknowledged the greeting. When a group of young bucks raised their beavers to her Brooke said, glancing at her indulgently once more, "You have most certainly livened up the existence of so many in this dull town," and she blushed.

A great number of people were strolling along the Grand Parade with its pleasant vista of the Avon and the surrounding hills. As always there was a group of people peering at the weir as the water tumbled its way down river.

The two riders carefully negotiated stationary carriages; there was certainly no room to ride other than sedately along the Grand Parade. Suddenly as they moved back into the side of the road after passing a carriage Clarinda froze in the saddle when her gaze indulgently raked the strollers. Her fingers tightened convulsively on the reins, causing her horse to stop. Her eyes opened wide in horror and she was obliged to stifle a cry at the sight of two men who appeared to be accosting and showing some small object to everyone they encountered.

Brooke rode on unknowingly for a few yards and then, giving her a puzzled glance, waited for her to catch up. She did urge on her horse then, but all the time her stare did not leave the two men. It was like a horrible dream come to life and she could scarce believe her eyes even though she knew she was wide awake, for ahead of them were none other than Sir Hector Liddell and his crony Lord Frampton.

As she groped for Brooke Pennington's arm she was sorely tempted to cry out in fear again. "It is my step-father!" she gasped. "Colonel Pennington, only look who is there!"

Their horses had all but come to a standstill in the road, but he looked not the least put out by her panic. In fact a faint smile was playing at the corners of his lips.

"I believe you are correct, Miss Devereaux," he answered in an odd tone.

It was almost triumphant, but Clarinda was too terrified to note it at that moment.

"We must turn around before they see us!" she urged.

"There is no use in such an action. Even if Sir Hector does not catch sight of you today he will discover you soon enough."

He was staring across at the two men as if waiting for recognition. Inevitably they were seen but it was Lord Frampton who noted their presence. The moment he did so his face lighted with triumph and he caught hold of his friend's arm. Sir Hector looked up, too. His expression changed quickly from one of surprise to anger.

During the few seconds in which this occurred Clarinda's heart beat with dread and in the midst of it all Brooke's attitude amazed her.

"What are we to do?" she wailed. "They have seen us. All is up."

He leaned towards her. "Do as I say and all will be well. Ride on as if nothing is amiss."

"I cannot. 'Tis impossible. He will kill me—you, too!"

"He will do nothing of the kind. We are in public view. Trust me and do as you're told, Clarinda. Ride. And don't speak to them in any circumstances. Do you understand? Whatever is said to either of us you must remain silent and allow me to speak for the both of us."

She nodded. It must have been his authoritative tone coupled with the use of her name which seemed to calm her a little and they rode on at a sedate pace as before.

When they came level with Sir Hector and Lord Frampton, Clarinda could scarce control the trembling of her limbs. It was all she could do to retain her seat. When it appeared they would ride past, the two men quickly stepped into the road in front of them.

"What is the meaning of this?" Brooke demanded.

A crooked smile came on to Sir Hector's face. In the months since she had left Birchwood, Clarinda had almost forgotten how loathsome he was.

"So my informant was correct after all," he said in triumph, and she realised he had in his hand a small miniature of her likeness.

To Clarinda's amazement Brooke sat back in the saddle and smiled. "Sir Hector Liddell if my memory serves me right."

The baronet stared malevolently at Clarinda all the while. "So she was with you that night."

"She?" Brooke glanced at Clarinda. "If you are referring to this young lady I must tell you I resent the implication, Sir Hector. This lady is a kinswoman of mine and a female of impeccable repute."

Sir Hector's face grew red and Clarinda stifled the wild desire to giggle.

"She is my step-daughter, sir!"

"And my betrothed," Lord Frampton added angrily, stepping forward to join the argument, which several people were witnessing with great delight.

"Hand her over to me," Sir Hector demanded. "I am bound to inform you that I am her legal guardian and she is under the age of her majority."

He reached out to pull Clarinda from the horse, which caused her to cry out at last. The horse started though, foiling Sir Hector's ploy for he was obliged to jump back.

Brooke Pennington, to Clarinda's further amazement, remained unperturbed. "Are you calling me a liar, sir?"

"I am, sir."

"I cannot tolerate such a slur on my honour. I must call upon you to answer to me in the manner normally employed by gentlemen."

At this Sir Hector looked triumphant once more. "I shall be delighted. We lodge in Queen Square."

Brooke nodded, grimly now. "My seconds will call upon you there as soon as possible."

Clarinda looked at him in bewilderment. "No!" she cried. "Brooke, not that. 'Tis not worth it."

Sir Hector transferred his attention to her then. "Colonel Pennington will soon discover for himself that you are not worth the fate awaiting him at my hands, and when I have despatched this cripple I will not delay in dealing with you, my girl."

She shuddered at the threat but her true concern, for Brooke's welfare, was a much greater one.

Giving her one last look of odium Sir Hector walked on, followed by Lord Frampton. Clarinda's eyes followed them, wide and full of fear.

Brooke took hold of the bridle and urged her horse on. She gave him a bewildered look and then turned once more to see that the two men were again standing in the middle of the road, staring after them.

At last she urged her horse into a canter to be out of their sight as soon as she could contrive. The moment they had passed into Bridge Street she cried, "You cannot really mean to fight a duel with him."

"Such matters are never spoken of lightly."

"I cannot believe that you are serious, though."

"It is arranged and there is no going back now."

He cast her a smile but she was by no means reassured by it. "Brooke, I know he is a crack shot. I also know he has fought duels before—and won them, too."

"So have I—and you may rest assured that I am held to be a good shot also."

"Oh, I beg of you retract. It will be no shame, for you did tell him an untruth. I couldn't bear it if he hurt you."

His face took on a stubborn look "You assume too much, my dear. There is nought amiss with my eye or my arm, even if my leg is less than perfect."

Fury tore at her then, directed against Lady Carlton whom she held to be the real culprit. "Oh, I know very well who informed him I am here! That abominable woman."

He glanced at her for the first time since their encounter with Sir Hector. "I don't know to whom you refer, but it was I who arranged for him to know your whereabouts."

At this revelation she almost fell off her horse, but then she spurred him on to catch up with Brooke. "You surely jest. You're gammoning me to protect her, are you not?"

"I have no cause to do so."

"Then why, oh why did you tell him?"

He glanced at her again. "You said yourself that you would never be free of him even once you were free of his guardianship. I deemed it best for you to face the consequences now rather than at some future time when you have allowed yourself peace of mind."

"Then you truly did contrive it," she realised at last. It was no jest after all. "That is why you took me riding today, so he should see us if he was abroad."

Her tone was reproachful. When he made no comment she cried in anguish, "Do you not realise he may kill you? He will not be satisfied with an exchange of shots, or even to draw the cork."

"Nor I, you may be certain." He smiled at her then as they entered the Crescent, as if they were discussing something of no real importance. "And you must, for your own sake, hope that it is I who is the victor."

Her eyes grew wide. "For my own sake! Oh, Brooke, do you not know me? Can I not persuade you to cry off?"

"No. There is nothing you can say which will do that, and I feel bound to warn you that Sir Hector will not; there is too much at stake."

When they reached Lady Pennington's house Clarinda immediately dismounted and ran to his horse, looking up at him appealingly as he sat tall and straight in the saddle. Just then he looked a fit match for Sir Hector, but she knew there was no possible way he could be, not on the ground.

"What can I say to you which will bring you to your senses? Can you not see I am out of my wits?"

He leaned forward in the saddle and gave her a comforting smile before putting one hand over hers.

"I truly regret causing you this anguish, Clarinda, but this duel is very necessary. I truly hope that the outcome will be as we both desire. Please forgive me."

He turned his horse and she watched him through misty eyes as he cantered away. Not until he had gone below the brow of the hill did she turn and walk dejectedly into the house, scarcely knowing how she would face Lady Pennington and Beth.

Twelve

"Is Brooke not coming in?" Beth asked, greeting Clarinda as she walked into the hall, cutting quite a different figure to the one who had run so joyously to greet him only a short time earlier.

Beth's tone of normality was just too much. Clarinda burst into tears which wracked her body.

Her friend's face took on a look of dismay as she put her arms around Clarinda's heaving shoulders.

"My dear, what is amiss? Has my foolish brother said something to put you out of countenance? I know from experience his tongue can be a mite sharp when he so chooses."

Her answer was to sob even louder until

a few moments later Lady Pennington appeared on the stairway, looking as concerned as her daughter.

"Clarinda! What can have happened to put you into such a taking?"

She hurried down the stairs and Clarinda sobbed, "My step-father is in Bath! It was Brooke who told him I am here. Now they're going to fight a duel and . . . it's all . . . my . . . fault!"

Lady Pennington drew back, her face growing pale. "A duel, you say, Brooke and Sir Hector Liddell?"

Clarinda nodded miserably. "I could not make him cry off. Oh, what are we to do?"

In a brisk voice Lady Pennington replied, "We cannot stand here discussing it in the hallway for all the servants to hear. Come along upstairs, into the drawing room."

She hurried Clarinda along, but Beth looked perplexed as she followed after. "Mama, what is this about?"

Once in the drawing room Lady Pennington thrust Clarinda on to the sofa and removed her hat. "There, that is better." She glanced around the room. "Now, where is my vinaigrette?"

"Pray do not trouble to find it," Clarinda told her, sitting up straight and blowing her nose on a wisp of lawn which served as a handkerchief.

"Mama," Beth insisted. "Would you be so kind as to tell me what *is* going on here?"

Lady Pennington looked to Clarinda who said in a flat voice, "Oh, do be pleased to tell her, ma'am."

In a low voice the older woman explained it all to her daughter who then drew in a sharp breath.

"I cannot credit this," she said, obviously amazed.

"'Tis perfectly true," Clarinda added, feeling discomfitted.

"And this is how Brooke's gallantry is to be rewarded." She cast a hate-filled look at Clarinda. "How I wish I had never clapped eyes upon you."

"Now, now," Lady Pennington said soothingly. "It is not Clarinda's fault."

"It is no one else's," Beth retorted.

"Beth, be silent!"

"She is correct," Clarinda murmured. "I am nought but a trial. I wish I had married Lord Frampton and then this situation could never have occurred."

"It is your fortune he requires, so it is not too late," Beth snapped. "You can still avert a catastrophe."

Clarinda stared at her for a moment or two before realising the girl was perfectly correct. The effect of those words made her immediately spring to her feet.

"Of course! Why did I not think of that? I shall go immediately and give myself up to Sir Hector's guardianship once again."

"And, mayhap, another beating," Lady Pennington pointed out as she gazed across the room at her.

"Do you really think I care about a mere beating if I can spare Brooke from worse harm?"

"Don't be such a chuckle-head," the lady scolded. "What will he say if you behave in such a foolish way?"

Clarinda gave her a curious look. "Lady Pennington, do you not wish to prevent this duel?"

"With all my heart, but I know in matters of honour we ladies must not interfere. It would not be appreciated, I assure you."

"It is not a matter of honour," Clarinda pointed out. "Sir Hector accused Brooke of lying, which he had done."

"Oh, Mama," Beth cried in exasperation, "why do you bandy words with her? Let her go to Sir Hector. If Brooke is angry it is of no consequence as long as he is *alive*."

"If only it were as simple as that, my dear. I fear that nothing Clarinda does will be of the slightest use. Her sacrifice on his behalf would be commendable, but it would make not the slightest difference to the situation, I fear."

She looked from one young lady to the other. "My dears, in these circumstances I am quite certain Brooke will forgive me for revealing something of which you are not aware."

She had their attention, even though Clarinda was obliged to sniff occasionally and dab at her eyes in a most unbecoming manner.

"Sir Hector is not entirely unknown to my son. I doubt if they have actually met before, but at Vimeiro the cowardice of a certain officer during the battle led to the deaths of many gallant men. There would have been many more, so I am told, if it were not for Brooke, who was obliged to go in and save them, which he did most heroically. That officer was Sir Hector Liddell, who was obliged to resign his commission soon after, and I know Brooke has always held him responsible not only for the carnage, but for his own injury."

Her words fell on stunned ears and at last

Clarinda said, "So it is not, after all, for my sake that he meets Sir Hector."

"You need suffer no guilt on that score, but I am quite persuaded, my dear, my son would have risen to your defence even had he not known of Sir Hector and his past deeds."

For some reason Lady Pennington's words did not comfort Clarinda as much as might be expected. At the realisation that this man whom she had come to love so much had probably used her plight to draw out Sir Hector for his own reasons, caused her to dissolve into tears once more.

Dawn was breaking at last, for the night had seemed endless. The sky was growing light and the birds indulging in their dawn chorus, but for once Clarinda found no charm in it. Her heart was filled only with dread for what the coming day would bring.

She had been unable to sleep. She had not expected to when the three downhearted ladies retired for the night. After a while she had risen again and lit a candle. She could not concentrate on Miss Austen's new novel either and so she had simply drawn back the curtains and watched for the dawn to approach.

When there came a faint knocking at the door she was already dressed, waiting for the news which she both longed for and dreaded.

Beth put her head around the door and after ascertaining that Clarinda was up she came in, clutching a candle in one hand and the shawl which covered her nightshift in the other.

"Somehow I thought you would be awake, too."

"How could I possibly sleep?" Clarinda asked wearily.

"May I come in?"

Clarinda cast her a wan smile. "I should be glad of the company. The waiting is intolerable."

Beth put down her candle and sat down on the bed. "Clarinda, I really am so very sorry I was beastly to you this afternoon."

"You said nothing which I did not already feel myself. Your mother's revelations have eased my conscience only a little, I fear. Whatever Brooke wished to do to Sir Hector, he would not have been able to act if I had not come upon the scene."

"If my brother is determined upon a course there is nought which will detract him from it." She got up again and peered out of the window. "Do you suppose it is done yet?"

"I don't know," Clarinda answered with a shudder, and then, looking earnestly, asked, "Do you believe Brooke can win?"

The girl looked woebegone. "He was always a crack shot, but his leg is a handicap I fear he cannot overcome."

"It is as I thought," Clarinda answered with a sigh. "Oh, heavens, why did he feel he had to defend me in this way?"

"Because he is a man of honour, I dare say."

"He is a giant amongst men, but I fear for his life."

Beth cast her an indulgent look then. "You love him, don't you?"

Clarinda could not meet her friend's frank look and instead turned to stare out of the window in the direction of Coombe Down.

"More than I ever believed possible."

"Men are such fools," Beth said harshly, and then sat down again.

"I would not deem him a fool. He gave his heart years ago and it is lost to him for ever."

"A fool is what he must be if he cannot see that you and he are a perfect match."

Clarinda smiled faintly. "Oh, my dear Beth, it is not for you to decide."

"I would dearly love you as a sister-in-law."

"It is no use if Brooke does not want me as a wife."

"As I said, men are such fools."

They were silent for a few moments and then Clarinda said with a sigh, "Poor Lady Pennington. How I feel for her agony."

Beth nodded. "I always felt Brooke was her favourite child, even though I know she would suffer equally for all of us in adversity."

"Not Sir Aubrey?"

The girl smiled. "You have yet to meet my elder brother. He is rather pompous as befits his situation, and Dulcie is so top-lofty, too. No, I am persuaded, Brooke is her favourite."

Suddenly both girls stiffened. "I am sure I can hear carriage wheels approaching," said Clarinda.

Beth jumped to her feet. "I am sure you are right, and who else would be coming in this direction at this hour?"

Of one accord they rushed out of the room and down the two flights of stairs. No servants yet stirred and it was Clarinda who drew back the bolt on the door and turned the key in the lock.

It must be Brooke, she said fervently to herself and Beth urged, "Oh, do hurry, Clarinda."

The door swung open as the carriage drew to a halt outside. Both Beth and Clarinda drew back in alarm, however, at the sight of Sir Hector's coat of arms on the door of the carriage which immediately burst open.

"Oh no!" Beth cried, her hands flying to her lips.

Clarinda cried out in alarm, too, as Lord Frampton climbed down. "Sir Hector has charged me with the task of fetching you, Clarinda," he said and his voice was low and guttural, sending shivers of apprehension down her spine.

Before he even came close to her she could smell the alcohol on him and guessed both he and her step-father had spent the night imbibing. When he advanced towards them both girls drew back into the hall.

"What has happened?"

It was Lady Pennington's fear-filled voice from the landing which caused them all to look up. She was clutching a shawl about her nightshift and looked pale and drawn.

There was no doubt she had also spent a sleepless night.

"Mourn your son, madam."

Lady Pennington fell back moaning. Clarinda cried out in grief and, uttering a groan, Beth rushed to lend succour to her mother.

Taking advantage of the confusion Lord Frampton caught hold of Clarinda's wrist and drew her from the house before the door could be slammed in his face. However, she did not struggle against him. Grief afflicted her too sorely to trouble. With Brooke dead her own fate was of no matter any longer.

He flung her unceremoniously into the carriage where she cowered in a corner, her mind filled only with images of Brooke lying dead on the dew-covered turf of Coombe Down. He climbed in after her, slamming the door behind him and fixing her with a steely look, of which she was only partly aware.

As the carriage jerked into motion he said, "Your step-father has entrusted you to my care. You should be thankful it is me and not him, for he is truly angry at the trouble to which he had been put of late. I trust you have learned the folly of your ways and will no longer resist the plans he has for your future."

"I don't care what happens to me any longer."

Lord Frampton sank back into the squabs as the carriage raced on. "Good. You may even learn to be glad. By the time we reach Gretna you will no doubt be eagerly anticipating our wedding which should have, by rights, taken place properly months ago. Such a shabby affair is your fault entirely."

Clarinda stared bleakly into space, such a prospect no longer striking terror in her heart which was too bruised to be further afflicted. She could only think that Brooke was dead and she would never see him again. After that she could only hope that death would not be long in claiming her, too. It was the only thing to which she could look forward with any enthusiasm.

Thirteen

The carriage jerked Clarinda out of her restless doze. For a few minutes at least she had been able to sink into oblivion and it had been welcome. At the immediate recollection, however, tears came to her eyes which she brushed away with an impatient hand lest he think her afraid of him.

"Where . . . are we?"

They could not have possibly reached Scotland yet, she reasoned.

"Not far enough," he confirmed, sounding grim, "but one of the horses has gone lame so we may as well refresh ourselves at this inn whilst the team is changed for a fresh one."

He took her wrist in his cruel grip and she said, "There is no need; there is nowhere to which I can run."

"Very true," he confirmed, sounding satisfied.

Even so he kept hold of her until they were inside the private parlour. The inn looked to be a shabby place, unused to serving the Quality. However, she was glad of the respite and went immediately to sit down in a corner as far away from him as possible. As he paced the floor restlessly she stared at him with defiance.

"The landlord is bringing us some food," he told her after a moment, "so I advise you to eat. After this we may not stop for some time to come."

Clarinda had not the slightest desire to

eat, but she said in a dull voice made rough by her tears, "I can readily understand that the sooner we are wed the quicker you and Sir Hector can put your hands on my fortune, but this undue haste is unnecessary. There is no one to pursue us." Once again her voice gave way beneath the weight of her grief.

"That is so, but this wedding has already been delayed an unconscionable time. I shall be more at ease once we are leg-shackled. Sir Hector is anxious for it to be done and at Gretna we need suffer no further delay."

"The duns must be becoming very insistent."

He cast her a furious look and just then the landlord and several of his lackeys came in bearing a cold collation and bottles of claret. When they had gone Lord Frampton tasted the wine carefully.

As he swallowed a glassful his face twisted into a grimace. "Inferior stuff, as I expected, but it will have to suffice."

"When we are wed," she taunted, "you will be able to afford the very best in wine."

"So shall we both, my dear," he answered, seemingly unperturbed.

He picked up a leg of chicken and began

to eat with gusto. Clarinda watched him in disgust as he ate and drank as quickly as he could, displaying no finesse. At last, after putting away an enormous amount of food, he wiped his greasy lips and looked at her again.

"Can I not persuade you to eat a morsel, my dear? There is more than enough for two."

Her answer was to shrink away. Heedless of her distaste he filled two glasses of wine.

"At least we must make a toast to our future life together. May it be a long and fruitful one."

As he held out the glass to her she dashed it from his hand and it crashed to the ground, shattering to fragments on the flags.

"There is no future for me."

Anger sparked in his eyes for the first time. "You foolish chit. Why do you persist in resisting me?"

"Why do you persecute *me?*"

"I have never treated you with anything other than high regard. I mean you no harm, Clarinda. Do you not know that I have always admired you?"

She turned her face from his. "This is an odd way of showing it."

"It is only a means to an end, you will see. I wish to give you jewels and clothes such as you've never seen before." He came closer to her, his voice slurred by the drink he had consumed. "I would make you a woman to be admired by all."

She flinched away from him and his breath which smelled of alcohol. "I am only a woman to be pitied."

He started with anger. "Other women find my attentions pleasant, why do you not?" When she made no reply, he asked in a harsh voice, "Is Pennington your lover?"

"He was a gentleman," she answered in a choked voice. "Something you wouldn't know anything about."

He drew away slightly. "My apologies, my dear. It was a foolish and impudent question, for it is obvious you would not take half a man as your lover, a proud beauty such as you."

Clarinda straightened up. "I would have been proud, I assure you. He was more of a man than you, Frampton."

"You impudent baggage . . ." he began angrily, causing her to flinch away from him once more.

He darted towards her, but suddenly he

stopped and straightened up, listening intently. Clarinda had no time to feel relief at the sudden respite before the door flew open and banged back against the wall.

Her eyes opened wide at the sight of Brooke in the doorway, his face almost black with fury.

"Hell and damnation!" swore Lord Frampton, looking frantically around for some weapon.

Clarinda was on her feet immediately. "Brooke, you're alive!" She turned on her captor then, fury tearing at her heart. "You told me he was dead! You said he was *dead!*"

As she raised her hand to beat him he caught her by the wrist and breathless, the earl taunted, "What do you expect to achieve, Pennington? A cripple like you cannot do anything to stop me."

"I can deal with you just as I dealt with your crony."

Lord Frampton let go of Clarinda's wrist and she shrank back, her hands to her lips as the earl advanced menacingly upon Brooke. However, he had taken only a few steps when Brooke lifted his cane. In the time it took her to blink he pulled it apart to reveal a wicked-looking blade which had been concealed inside.

Lord Frampton paused then, weighing the odds a little more carefully now. As he did so Brooke said, breathless with anger, "Do not doubt I would use this, Frampton. It would be my pleasure to do so, I assure you." The earl still hesitated and Brooke jabbed the sword-stick in the direction of the door where several of the inn servants dallied. "Your horses are put to, Frampton, so take my advice and be gone whilst you are still hale and hearty. I don't wish to clap eyes upon you ever again, and I know Miss Devereaux echoes my feelings."

After hesitating only a moment longer, the earl went past him, giving Clarinda one last look. She closed her eyes in a silent prayer of thankfulness and then went on unsteady legs to Brooke as he slid the blade back into its shaft, rendering the cane harmless once again.

Her eyes were shining now as the sound of the earl's carriage faded into the distance, out of her life for ever.

"He said you were dead," she repeated in a choked voice.

She took his face between her hands, looking upon the features she had despaired of seeing again.

"It was his last desperate chance to marry

you." Her hair had tumbled to her shoulders. He reached out and touched it tenderly before taking hold of her arms and gazing at her hard. "He has not hurt you?"

His voice was harsh and insistent. Clarinda shook her head, oblivious to her ordeal now.

"He had more need of my fortune than anything else."

At this he smiled. "I always considered him to be more of a fool than a knave and now I know it is true."

They gazed at each other for a long moment. "Oh, Brooke, it's so wonderful to see you," she sighed.

He drew her closer to him then and her heart began to beat fast. "What a fright you gave me."

His lips brushed her cheek, causing her heart to flutter in an even wilder manner than before. "I . . . but I thought *you* . . ."

Her words were lost as he cradled her in his arms. "It doesn't matter. It's all over. You have nothing left to fear."

She remained motionless in his arms, comforted by his closeness. After a few moments he held her away, searching her face. Her heart began to flutter again as she whispered his name, knowing that suddenly his attitude had changed. He was no longer looking at her in his usual avuncular way; the atmosphere between them was charged.

"Clarinda," he whispered, drawing her close again.

When his lips found hers she surrendered to his kiss with a passion she could not have guessed she possessed until that moment. She had no notion how long they stood there clasped in each other's arms, trading kiss for feverish kiss, but that ramshackle hostelry was the most heavenly place on earth.

Only when someone clearing his throat intruded did they part and Clarinda experienced a deep pain at the loss of his touch. Brooke gave her a long look and she turned away, feeling bashful as the landlord bowed to them both.

"A carriage has arrived, m'lord."

He looked at them both curiously but Clarinda felt only elation, the triumph of a love not only freely given but one which was also returned.

Then she suddenly became alarmed and her hands flew to her lips.

"It must be Sir Hector."

Brooke shook his head. "Impossible. More like Mama's carriage with your maid to accompany you. We shall travel back to

Bath immediately. Come. We have stayed at this place far too long."

He threw a purse on to the table. "For your trouble, landlord."

As the landlord rushed to count his treasure Clarinda hurried to follow Brooke outside. He had suddenly become withdrawn from her and not at all lover-like. Nothing could detract from the wonder of his kisses, but his manner now did hurt and puzzle her.

"Brooke, I beg of you tell me what happened this morning. Did you kill Sir Hector?"

"I think not. I shot him in the leg." He put his hand over where his own wound must have been. "Just here."

She stared at him in wonder and he went on, smiling slightly. "You must wonder how it came about."

"No, no," she was quick to assure him.

He continued to smile. "You will not be alone, I assure you, but when a man suffers a disability such as mine he is determined to succeed in as many fields as possible. That is what your step-father overlooked. Mayhap, he will discover it for himself now."

She hardly knew what to say, but then

declared, "Oh, poor Lady Pennington! Does she know you are safe?"

He laughed then. "Yes, she knows."

"I fear she was dreadfully shocked when Lord Frampton told her you were dead."

"And now she is in a fidge lest I not find you."

"How could she doubt it? But I am at a loss to know how you were so close behind us."

"It is not such a puzzle. Immediately after the duel, when Sir Hector was lying on the ground, he whispered something to Frampton who shot off in the carriage as if all the Furies were after him. It suddenly occurred to me that he was up to no good, and I set off in pursuit.

"I arrived at Royal Crescent only minutes after he had set off with you, to discover Mama in a swoon, the household in total chaos, and you gone. At this point it seemed obvious that his destination must be Gretna if he wished to secure a right to your affairs so I set off in pursuit once more."

"So again I have cause to be grateful to you."

"For the last time. Sir Hector Liddell is no longer a threat to your well-being. He will not seek to harm you now, for even if he were able he has not the means. That leg of his will take a long time to heal."

Kate got out of Lady Pennington's carriage and when she caught sight of Clarinda, exclaimed, "Oh, thank the Lord you're safe! You might have been harmed—even killed. Come inside the carriage, do, ma'am, afore you catch your death."

"Oh, do stop fussing, Kate," Clarinda replied. "I am perfectly robust, as you can see."

Brooke eyed her wryly. "I feel it only fair to tell you that all those at Royal Crescent are in a worse taking than you."

She laughed as he handed her into the carriage and her heart was light once more.

Fourteen

"Really, Clarinda, you will have to come out of the dismals, you know."

Beth looked at her friend critically. "You look quite done up despite being dipped every day for a month."

They were in Lady Pennington's carriage, returning from the Pump Room. Clarinda knew her spirits were depressed but as she had not seen Brooke since the day of the duel she could not force herself in a mood of gaiety however many diversions she attended. She missed his presence dreadfully and knew that true happiness was not possible for her until she could be with him again.

"You must recall," Lady Pennington explained, "poor Clarinda suffered a terrible ordeal at the hands of that dreadful man. I am only glad she did not contract a brain fever as a result of it. I am persuaded it could easily have been so." She leaned forward slightly. "I am sure you are consoled by the knowledge that Sir Hector Liddell has received his reward for all his past deeds and that Brooke is quite safe."

Clarinda smiled wanly. "Indeed I am, Lady Pennington."

"I wonder when Brooke will return," Beth mused. "He has been gone an unconscionable time."

"Recall that duels are not allowed in law," her mother pointed out. "It was prudent of him to leave Bath when he did. Indeed, I doubt if he will return at all this year. We may not see him again until we are in London next month."

Every word she spoke was like a blow to Clarinda's heart.

"I would have thought he might have returned for a short stay at least," Beth mused, and then in a bright voice, "I have today discovered that Lord Tetbury is to come to London, too! He told me of it when we met in the Pump Room. Is that not good news?"

Clarinda managed a smile. "I am so pleased for you, Beth. His regard for you has certainly grown of late."

The girl sighed. "I am persuaded there is now a chance he will come up to scratch, only he is a man who likes to take his time. I am not yet come out. I feel I can afford to wait." She looked at Clarinda. "Men do like to be certain about such an important matter," she added, which caused Clarinda to blush. "They are not so impulsive as females, especially when it comes to giving something so important as a heart."

"It seems," her mother said, with some satisfaction, "you are becoming sensible at last. I am quite looking forward to the masquerade at the Sydney Gardens tonight."

"Oh yes, indeed," Beth echoed as the carriage laboured up the hill into the Crescent.

The girl's eyes were bright and her friend was certain she was anticipating a chance meeting in the shrubbery with Lord Tetbury. Clarinda fervently hoped that this was one romance which would end happily.

"Clarinda, we have a surprise for you," Lady Pennington announced when they entered the house.

Clarinda looked at her hopefully as, giggling, Beth handed her two packages.

"It is your birthday! Have you forgotten?"

Clarinda had scarce given a thought to the fact that she had come of age, once a most important event, but even so her fingers fumbled anxiously with the string.

"Do you recall the day you went riding with Brooke?" Beth asked breathlessly.

"Shall I ever forget it?"

"Buying your gift was my errand. You never guessed, did you?"

The paper parted to reveal a silk shawl. "Oh, it is so beautiful," Clarinda cried. "Thank you; thank you so much."

She hugged Beth and then began to open the smaller package which contained an enamelled trinket box. Clarinda's eyes filled with tears of gratitude.

"Lady Pennington, I am overwhelmed. How lovely it is and how kind of you to remember."

"The gifts are only a small token of our affection for you, my dear. You are now a very wealthy young woman."

As Lady Pennington took off her bonnet, Clarinda reflected that she should have been the happiest of females, but the one person to make that happen was miles away.

They had just been divested of their outdoor clothes when the door to the downstairs parlour opened. All three ladies turned on their heels.

"You females spend an unconscionable time chattering," Brooke declared as he paused in the doorway.

Both Lady Pennington and her daughter rushed forward to embrace him.

"This is a splendid surprise!" his mother declared and Clarinda hovered shyly in the hall. "When did you arrive?"

"Late last night."

"You should have sent a note to warn us. Surprises are not good for one of my advanced years."

"Tush, Mama," her daughter contradicted, "surprises such as this are delightful."

He was looking past them now across at Clarinda. "Do you not wish to greet me?"

She forced a smile to her lips. "Of course

I do. I am delighted to see you, Colonel Pennington."

He raised an eyebrow at her formality and Lady Pennington said, "You must take a dish of tea with us, Brooke, and dinner, of course. I shall go and speak with Cook to apprise her of the extra person. In the meantime, Clarinda, take Brooke in the drawing room and inform him of all the news since he left."

"What a splendid notion," Beth agreed. "Come along, Brooke."

However as she stepped forward Lady Pennington caught her arm. "Beth dear, did you not tell me not many moments ago that you need to complete your mask for the masquerade ball this evening?"

The girl bit her lip and nodded. "What a chuckle-head I am! I had quite forgotten in all the excitement of the moment." She touched her brother's arm. "We will talk later."

When they had both gone Clarinda made to walk up the stairs, feeling all at once discomfited at being alone with him, although it was what she yearned for above all else. Before she had reached the bottom step, however, he moved rather briskly towards the front door, which still remained open.

"I suspect that dish of tea may be some time in arriving. Mayhap a turn in Crescent Fields will be more beneficial." He frowned in her direction. "You look a trifle peaked, Clarinda. I do trust your ordeal does not affect you still."

"I am perfectly well, I thank you."

She walked with him across the road and down the path into the Fields which afforded them an unparalleled view of the town.

"I have some rather distressing news to impart," he said after a moment. "It is as well for me to speak of it first." She looked at him, feeling dread as he stared across the town. "Your step-father died last week."

Whatever she had expected him to say, it was certainly not this and she gasped. "But he was only wounded . . . his leg . . . you said so . . ."

"He was not as fortunate as I, it appears. For one thing he insisted on travelling to London soon afterwards and as a result lost a good deal of blood. Then the wound became infected because of ineffectual treatment, by quacks, no doubt. All further efforts to save him were in vain."

"Will you be brought to book for his death?"

"No. The matter is finished. There is nothing to fear from that direction."

That at least afforded her some relief. She looked down at the grass beneath her feet, attempting to make some sense of her own thoughts.

At last she said, "He was not a good man and although I did not wish any real harm to come to him, in all honesty I cannot be sorry."

"Even with your innate goodness, I would not expect such magnanimity." After a moment he went on, "More happily I can tell you I have taken the liberty of calling upon your father's lawyer and he informs me that there will be no difficulty in transferring your property to yourself. Only a few signatures are required to achieve your independence and he will be happy to call upon you the moment you arrive in London."

"You are so very good," she murmured, aware that he was watching her carefully.

"I had hoped to find you more happy."

"You may be sure that I am, never more so."

"I know it is your birthday today. Did

you think I had forgotten?" She looked at him then, hating the return of that avuncular tone. "I hope you'll accept this small token from me to mark the occasion."

He brought a velvet box from his pocket and opened it. Nestling against the satin was a bracelet made up of small emeralds. Clarinda gasped and her face immediately brightened.

"It's lovely."

When she made no move to touch it he removed it from the box and fastened it around her wrist.

As she gazed at it she said, "But it is far too valuable . . ."

"It bears little value compared to what you will one day possess."

"Nothing will be as precious to me as this," she answered, gazing at him longingly.

To her chagrin he began to walk on. "You must know that Mama wishes to take you to London and present you."

"Yes, she has mentioned it to me. It is very kind of her but I don't wish for a Season. It's too late."

"What will you do?" he asked her, frowning as she hastened to join him once more.

"Once I have clarified my affairs with the

lawyer there will be no reason why I cannot return to Birchwood. It was always a happy place before Sir Hector became the master. I shall enjoy living there again just as I was always used to do."

"You plan to live there alone?"

She laughed harshly. "Yes."

He stopped, looking at her intently once more. "You really should allow my mother to present you. You must make friends, allow men to pay court to you, and eventually marry."

"If I cannot have you I want no one," she burst out, beyond all care now. "Do you not know I love you, Brooke?" He looked away again, causing her untold pain. "When we were at that inn I thought you might love me, too."

Her eyes pleaded with him and when he sighed her hopes were dashed completely.

"Clarinda, you are young, beautiful and wealthy. There is no position so high you cannot aspire to it. Besides, what use am I to a woman like you?"

She gasped. "You chuckle-head. There is nothing you cannot do. You have proved beyond all doubt that you are not only equal to all men, but better than most."

"I cannot dance," he answered, giving her a wry smile.

"Do you truly believe I wish to spend the rest of my life dancing? I'd as lief be with you at Cressfield Manor, or at Birchwood, even here in Bath, as long as I am *with you.*"

He put both hands on her arms. "You have suffered a great deal of late . . ."

Angrily she retorted, "Do you treat every woman who falls in love with you as if she has windmills in her head? Oh, Brooke, do you think you could let Amelia's memory fade enough to love me a little, too? 'Tis all I would ask of you."

His eyes narrowed slightly. "Amelia?"

"I know how much you loved her, and love her still, but all I want is to be with you. I shall not ask for that kind of devotion. 'Tis enough I can be devoted to you."

He shook his head. "What foolish notions. Of course Amelia was dear to me, but you may be certain you are no less dear."

Her heart surged with happiness. "Then why are you so aloof to me? There is no reason for us to be apart."

"Are you certain it is what you want? 'Tis not gratitude . . . ?"

"I shall always be indebted to Lady Pennington but you did not seek to protect me from Sir Hector for my own sake. You used me to feed your desire for revenge. As you once said to me, you have cause to be grateful to me," she reminded him wryly.

"That isn't precisely true although I confess I did welcome the chance of crossing his path again."

He took her hands in his and raised them to his lips. "I truly believe I loved you from the first. I wanted you as a part of my life from the moment I clapped eyes on you."

His face was very close to hers, searching her features as if they were new to him. Regardless of others strolling in the Fields, he drew her into his arms. She sighed with contentment as he whispered, "I love you," into her ear, his lips caressing her neck.

Then, as she trembled with anticipation, his lips found hers and he began to kiss her with a relentless passion which left her breathless.

When he released her she was dismayed and went once again into his arms.

"You are shameless," he told her but with evident delight.

"I have lived with uncertainty for so long I must keep reassuring myself this is not a dream. However, I vow I shall renounce my hoydenish ways and become more demure as befits my new station in life."

He laughed. "Not too demure, I beg of you."

Happily she slipped her hand into his free one, but he immediately withdrew his, reaching into his pocket once more.

"You may as well have this, too."

It was a smaller box, one which contained an emerald ring, matching the bracelet. Her eyes were bright as he extracted it from the satin and slipped it on her finger.

"It is most suited to you, even though the gem is dulled by the brightness of your eyes."

"You knew all along," she murmured.

"I hoped," was his reply as he raised the beringed hand to his lips, "but not too highly, I own."

She laughed, saying, "And all the while I was in despair."

"That is something firmly in the past for both of us, my love."

He took her hand in his then and together they walked back up the Fields to break the happy news to Beth and Lady Pennington, unaware that the two ladies were standing at the drawing room window gleefully regarding the lovers as they returned.